Digital Voodoo

The collected short works of:

Timothy O. Goyette

ISBN: 069259714X
ISBN-13: 978-0692597149

Cover art by Chris Goyette
gemstonehelix@mail.com

CONTENTS

Acknowledgments

I would like to acknowledge the support of family, fellow writers and the gang at Quantum Muse.

Foreword

by Andrew Baker

The short story and the short story author have a difficult job to do. It's no easy feat to set a story, imagine and transfer the results of your imagining artistically into words, and to do it using far less paper, while accomplishing the same level of creative story telling as a full size book. Charged with leading the literary section of FanboysAnonymous.com, I've had the privilege of meeting and speaking with a great number of authors. An interesting and defining quality I've noticed in a certain, particularly skilled, author is his affinity for short stories and short story telling. His Quantum Muse E-zine is a perfect example.

Having read and reviewed "Lockdown", a Timothy Goyette major work, I was introduced to his various links, Quantum Muse most importantly, which hosts contests for serious science fiction short story writers and artists and collects donations to help these creators keep producing their work. For me, and I'm sure for many, the Quantum Muse E-zine stands out as one of the greatest indie platforms on the web. For those of us writing indie work, such platforms are too far and few. It's one thing to experience the hardship of trying to be a successful author, but to build a creative outlet based on that hardship; one that allows for the hidden gems to rise and be heard, is entirely different. Finally, in a world filled with injustice, there stands a hero against the villainy of corporate literary crime.

Timothy, being the fanatic that he is for short works, has written many science fiction short stories. This new collection of short stories by Timothy O. Goyette plays an odd game with its readers that I appreciate and I'm sure you will too. I float through life in such a state of mind that I thought perhaps my mind was rearranging these stories for my entertainment. Though, upon second read, it would appear they are ordered in such a way that causes them to run together, almost as if part of a schizophrenic dream. These shorts set an odd cloud of amnesiac déjà-vu upon me, which is a unique reminder that perhaps there are people just as weird as myself out there. It's a feeling that I've experienced through just one other medium in life; a television show that no longer exists, but that everyone still remembers, called The Twilight Zone. I hope you appreciate this series of shorts as much as I have. Sweet schizophrenic dreams.

Humorous Stories:

The first four stories are tales of Sasha and Katrina. I enjoy writing these two characters as they tend to write themselves. The stories are presented in chronological order and show how the characters have evolved.

It's Your Hair

"Look at her," said Sasha.

Katrina, the blond Amazon, glanced over her shoulder. "What, the bar maid?"

Sasha lifted the helm off her head and slammed it on the table. Their dishes rattled with the force. "Half the men in the place are falling over each other trying to get next to her."

"Men are like that, always chasing after some fluff."

"Haven't you ever wanted a man?"

Katrina looked at her companion with a smirk and raised her eyebrows.

"That's not what I mean. You know, settle down on a farm, or something, and raise children? A life with a good, hard working, loving, man."

"Of course not! I was born with a brain."

A voice came from behind Sasha. "And how are you girls tonight?" It was the slurred speech of a drunken sod.

Katrina scrunched her face in disgust and shook her head. Sasha didn't have to look to tell it was an old, one-toothed, dirty, fat jerk who had one too few drinks which was made obvious because he was able to stand and speak. These louts were only good company when they were unconscious. A hand came to rest on her bare shoulder.

"Maybe I can show you girls around?"

Sasha leaned forward, pulling her chair onto the front two legs. She scooted back just a bit, and slammed a chair leg down on the lout's foot. He opened his mouth to shout, but she stifled it with an elbow to the head. He fell to the ground unconscious.

Sasha leaned in to her companion. "Why don't men find me attractive?"

Katrina rested her chin on her fist and looked with her head cocked to the left. After a moment, she leaned back with a smile. "It's your hair."

Sasha ran a hand down the tight braid at the back of her head. "Do you really think so?"

"Of course, look at the barmaid. Men are drawn to women who look wild, untamed."

"But, I am wild and untamed!"

"Yes, but you don't look it. You keep your hair tied back all the time."

"I have to - it keeps it out of the way during battle."

"You're not in a battle now," Katrina said with a wink.

"You never know when one's going to spring up."

"Go ahead, let your hair down."

Sasha scanned the room. No one was watching, although she was certain everyone was. They just looked down when she glanced their way.

"Come on Sasha, you'd eat with your hands, belch, or cut someone open right in front of anyone here, without a care. Why should your hair matter?"

"I haven't worn it down since I was a child. What if Recter, or Baffet were to come in?"

"They haven't noticed we're women in the past three years, they're not going to start now."

Sasha pulled her braid around her neck. It was long enough to reach past her collarbone. She fidgeted with the cord binding the braid. The strong leather cord was lashed about the trunk of hair and tied in a double knot. "Darn this knot," she said picking at the edges.

"So, now you want long nails too? You are turning into a girl."

"Shut up," Sasha hissed. The venom in her voice would have chased a wolverine from its dinner.

Katrina stood up, shoving her seat back. The scraping sound exploded in Sasha's ears. "Do you have to make such a fuss? Now everyone's looking." Although no one looked away from their drinking, laughing, or talking. Sasha lowered her head and surveyed the room from the corners of her eyes.

"Let me have that," Katrina said, taking the knot. "No, I've changed my mind."

"Don't be a baby about it. You'll be beautiful in no time."

Sasha heard the slicing sound of a knife leaving its scabbard. She groped behind her, grasping for the hair.

The dull sound of cutting came while she felt a tug on her hair. "Stop it," she shouted, jumping to her feet. She turned on Katrina who stood smiling with the remnant of leather cord in her hand.

"Quiet," Katrina shushed as she headed back to her chair. "You'll make a jester of yourself."

Looking around, all the nearby tables had grown silent, and faces turned to her. She rushed back into her chair and lowered her head. "Katrina, one time in your future, you will regret this."

"Ha, it's not like the time Felven sat on that ant hill," Sasha smiled despite herself.

"Never seen a man take his pants off so fast."

Sasha's smile grew. "Right in front of his holiness and the prince."

"It was the best job we ever lost."

"But it was worth it!" The two broke into raucous laughter. The people around them turned their attention back to their own business.

Sasha reached up to brush aside a hair that had fallen loose during her revelry. Her hand stopped at the ear. It felt vaguely familiar. She looked up to

Katrina.

"Come on woman, shake it out."

The corner of Sasha's mouth twisted up into her most mischievous grin. "The devils be drowned," she called hoisting her mug aloft. Katrina's came crashing into it as she echoed the toast.

Sasha shook her head with the force of a cornered viper. The braids broke loose and waves of hair came crashing over her ear. The mass of hair encircled her face, framing it and softening.

Katrina stopped laughing. "You really do look different."

Sasha laughed louder. The deed was done and she'd slash the first to make jest of her.

"Katrina," a male voice boomed over the din. A beefy arm waved over the crowd. She waved back. Baffet made his way between the tables and stumbling patrons. He dragged a chair out from under someone who wouldn't notice it missing.

"Hey Katrina, who's your friend?" His broad hand pushed back his greasy hair.

A gorilla goes mating, was all Sasha could think of. Pressing her lips into a smile, she held in the snickering. Across the table, Katrina placed a hand over her mouth.

Baffet even excused himself for burping. "And, what is your name, lovely lady?"

Katrina broke first, her fist slamming the table amid her gasps for breath. Sasha followed immediately after. Baffet's expression of confusion only added to their mirth.

Only when Baffet got up to leave did Sasha squeeze out, "Baffet you fool, it's me."

He looked and looked again. He grabbed a handful of hair that covered part of her face and moved it aside. "Sasha, that really you? In the name of Eros, do you look different? I mean, I never ..." He coughed a couple of times.

Sasha kicked his seat. "Get over it, you great beast. Sit down and drink."

He sat down with a thud. "You're not the Sasha that wipes gore from her blade on her opponent's dead bodies. What'd you do? Been flirting with dark magic?"

"Here, have a drink." Sasha shoved her mug in front of the oaf. "Now then, what's the news with the others?"

He sat like a lump, rubbing his forehead and staring at Sasha. "What is it?"

"You look different, really different. I've never thought about it before."

"Well, don't now," Sasha said fiddling with her dagger. "We didn't invite you, but we can un-invite exceptionally well."

A new voice entered the conversation. "Is this peasant bothering you, m'lady?"

Sasha looked up into sea green eyes, chiseled features and flowing blond hair. Katrina whistled then winked at Sasha. Sasha opened her mouth to explain that Baffet was a well-meaning idiot, whom they were willing to put up with, but Baffet cut her off.

"She don't need any help from a pretty boy like you. Now, be gone."

The stranger moved fast. Before she could suck in her breath, he had drawn his rapier. The tip flashed across the table and stopped at Baffet's throat. "Let's hear from the lady, shall we?"

Baffet swallowed and nodded his head. The stranger turned to Sasha. "I am Niles Townsend, at your service." He gave a slight bow, keeping his point under control. "What say you? Should I dispatch this braggart?"

Baffet's brow wrinkled. "Well, tell him..." The tip of the blade pressing against his throat ended his sentence.

Sasha decided to play this out for a while longer. Baffet deserved some humiliation. He considered those fancy lightweight weapons, and the whelps that wielded them, as fodder. It would give them many wonderful campfires reliving his time at the end of a frog stick.

Katrina kicked her under the table. Her eyes said: "Talk to the man, before I do."

She looked up at Niles. He was handsome and young. His clothes were not the tattered rags of the assembled multitude. A young adventurer, probably hiring his services as body guard to a local noble or something.

Sasha smiled. "Dear sir," she struggled for words. "This lout, as you so goodly called him, is..."

The blood drained from her face as she jumped up yelling, "No!"

It was too late; the pommel of a short sword came down on the back of the young man's head. Behind him was the smiling face of Recter.

"What do you think you are doing?" she glared, throwing poisoned darts from her eyes.

Recter's smile melted into confusion.

Katrina was up, looking down at Niles. "We lose the best ones that way."

A shout rose from behind Recter. "They're attacking the prince!" Katrina mumbled out the word, "Prince?"

"Katrina!" Sasha yelled just before the room fell into chaos. Tables were over turned, chairs were flying and the ringing of steel melded with shouting as a melee ensued.

Sasha clamped down on Katrina's wrist, holding her sword arm. "No you don't. We're getting out of here."

"But," Katrina said before being silenced by the vicious intensity of Sasha.

They worked their way to the door, avoiding injury from the seething mass of mayhem. Finally, at the door Sasha let go of Katrina's hand. Sasha immediately entwined her fingers into her hair and began weaving. To Katrina's questioning glance she responded. "This is the last time you'll talk me into one of your hair brained ideas."

Was It My Turn to Put Out the Rats?

"This won't hurt, Mr. Whiskers," Katrina said as she wrapped her fingers around the pudgy body of her favorite rat.

"You shouldn't make friends with those wretched creatures," Sasha said. She moved in with the syringe. "Just hold it still, will you?"

"You aren't vermin, Mr. Whiskers, are you?" Katrina touched noses with the sniffing rodent.

"Don't make me sick."

"Do you ever wonder what we're putting into our furry friends?"

"If it were really important they'd have one hundred thousand dollar-a-year scientists working on it in some secret lab in New Mexico. Let's not get carried away."

"But, what if we're filling my sweet baby with cancer causing agents?" Katrina turned Mr. Whiskers to face Sasha. "How could you hurt a face like this?"

"With a shovel. Now hold him still."

"Oh well, time for your medicine Mr. Whiskers."

The experienced hands inserted the needle, delivered the fluid and withdrew with a flick. Mr. Whiskers didn't seem to notice.

Katrina, with a sparkle in her eye, looked up at her dark haired friend. "Doctor Mortimer must have a file in his office on this experiment."

"No, no, no. You're not dragging me into another stupid adventure!"

"He claims to have an open door policy. He says we can come see him anytime we need help."

"That's not what he meant."

"Don't do it for the adventure, me, or even them." Katrina waved an arm towards the cages. "Do it for yourself. What kind of peace of mind can you have knowing you've killed these little creatures, and not know if it is truly worth it?"

"Six fifty an hour, we're not paid enough to care."

"It would help my peace of mind." Katrina's face sank to doleful pleading.

"You're going to keep this up until I give in aren't you?"

Katrina's smile became devious.

"Okay, let's get this over with."

"Good. Come on Mr. Whiskers."

"You're not bringing that along?"

"He has a right to know what he's dying for, doesn't he?"

With a sigh, Sasha swung her arms to the door. "Shall we?"

They closed the lab door behind them. The hall was dark. Bright streaks and splotches filtered in from street lights, through storage rooms and labs. The floors of the venerable building creaked under their weight.

Mr. Whiskers stood on Katrina's shoulder, sniffing at the air.

Sasha broke the silence. "It's nice you brought that rat along."

"You hear that Mr. Whiskers, Sasha likes you."

"Yeah, right. If we run into anything that the rat doesn't scare away, we can sacrifice the little beast to it."

"Cover your ears Mr. Whiskers; you don't want to hear things like that."

As if in response, the white rodent squeaked a high howl and jumped from Katrina's shoulder. Both women watched in stunned silence as the skinny tail disappeared under the archeology storage room door.

Katrina turned to Sasha; her mouth twisted into an apologetic smile. "Oops."

"You realize what will happen if we don't get that creature back? The test will be ruined; we'll be fired, and maybe expelled, if we're lucky."

Katrina was the first to the door. The knob rattled as she violently turned it one way, then the other. "Oh, great, it's locked."

She knelt down, putting her face to the floor. "Mr. Whiskers," she called under the door.

Sasha pulled a flat piece of metal from her pocket, and inserted it into the keyhole.

The rattling caused Katrina to look up. "Give it up Sasha, you can't pick a lock."

"These ancient ones are more of a challenge, but it should be..." The handle turned and the door opened. "Voila."

Katrina stood up. "When did you learn to do that?"

"Ryan Miller, a guy from high school, his father was a lock smith." Sasha said as she headed into the room.

"Why didn't you tell me before? You know what we can do with this?"

"Sorry girl, I only use my powers for good. Except once, but that was a special case."

Katrina raised her eyebrows.

"Guy Velmouth."

"That was you?"

They walked past row upon row of shelving. Dusty boxes, books, and occasional artifacts filled the room from ceiling to floor.

"Well," Katrina pleaded, "give, give."

"I was dancing with him at this party."

"Ooh..." Katrina said looking down an aisle.

"Yeah, until Susie Hatchmiere walked by. She flashed her baby blues and he was gone. Bang, just like that, and I was left standing on the dance floor alone."

"Justifiable homicide," Katrina's voice

seethed.

"Un huh," Sasha intoned.

"But still, I think you went overboard on revenge."

"Maybe a little," Sasha shrugged.

A squeak came from further back in the room.

"Sh…," Sasha shushed holding up her hand.

There was a faint glowing beyond the next row of shelving. The two women edged around to the aisle. Near the end, Mr. Whiskers lay on his belly and squeaked quietly. Before him was a miniature shrine, the size you'd expect to see under a Christmas tree. It was dirty and pieces were obviously missing from the twisted root that it must have been carved from. An aura shone around it, bluish white, with occasional flashes of green.

The two women stared at each other, fumbling for words. The squeaking fell into a rhythm.

"A chant?" asked Katrina.

"Look, we have an escaped lab rat. Stay focused on that. Block everything else out."

Katrina rolled her eyes in amazement. "How can I not…"

Sasha cut her off. "I'll circle around to the other side. It'll be trapped between us. We grab it and go. Don't look back."

Sasha left her open-mouthed friend and hurried down the next aisle. From the other side she was much closer to the escapee. Katrina, at the other end, seemed to have more control of herself now.

The two closed in on the prone animal. Sasha scooped it up and sprinted towards her friend.

One step, two steps, Sasha closed to within an arm's length of Katrina. A light, like a dozen flashbulbs, exploded behind Sasha.

Katrina blinked furiously, trying to clear the white fog from her sight. Sasha grabbed her wrist. "What have you done now?"

"Me? You're the one who grabbed the rat."

A high-pitched voice, too high to boom, boomed. "Let my pilgrim go."

Sasha ripped her hand away from Katrina.

Again the voice boomed, "Let my pilgrim go!"

"I think he means Mr. Whiskers, Sasha."

"Oh!" Sasha dropped the rat and turned. Before them stood a seven-foot tall rat. Its white fur was as inviting as that of a baby seal's. Mr. Whiskers scurried to the figure and climbed up the giant. He nestled, blanketed in the white fluff on his host's shoulder.

The huge beast cracked a caricature smile gazing on the little rat.

Sasha put her arm around Katrina and tiptoed away from the apparition.

"Wait, humans. Why have you tortured my children?"

Katrina spoke up. "We aren't torturing them. We look after them, like at a country club."

"This pilgrim says that you are kind, although given to silliness and undignified behavior with his kin. But you," It said looking at Sasha, "torture them with all sorts of picking and probing, leaving many of them sick."

Sasha cleared her throat. "I'm just trying to help."

"You keep them locked up, prisoners."

"No, no," Katrina responded. "Those are condos, luxury apartments. Look, I don't know what Mr. Whiskers has been telling you, but all the others are happy with their accommodations."

"That's right," Sasha added. "They are fed regularly and want for nothing."

"Except freedom. My disciples need to roam, to scurry about. Can they come and go as they please?"

"We let them out regularly for exercise." Katrina crossed her fingers behind her back.

"So, they have been out today?" the monster hissed as it stepped closer.

The two women looked at each other. Katrina shrugged.

Sasha looked from Katrina to the creature. "Was it my turn to put out the rats? Maybe this once…"

"Enough! Take me to my subjects!"

The women turned and started walking. As they rounded the corner, they sprinted for the door. Two strides into flight they were thrown to the ground. Their bodies flopped to the wooden floor; their arms and legs lay limp.

"What is this thing?" Sasha asked looking up at the giant rodent.

"I am the god of nature," it beamed with pride.

"The god of nature is a 7 foot tall rat?" Katrina asked.

"Yeah, I thought it was Mother Nature."

"Humans," the god of nature said in disgust. He focused his gaze on each of them. In turn, they regained control of their limbs. "Now, lead on."

Sasha and Katrina entered the lab. They gingerly made their way opposite the door, by the windows.

The great beast lumbered in, cocooned in silence. It scanned the room quickly. Its fur turned gray and bristly. The perfect white teeth yellowed. Its pink eyes burned red. "Let my people go!"

Both women were too stunned to move.

A shrill screech shot out from the god of nature, shattering all the glass within the room. Katrina and Sasha clamped their hands over their ears.

Objects began flying about the room, first papers and pencils, followed by a throng of books, cages and furniture. In the center, Mr. Nature morphed. His fur, matted and dense, stuck out from his body in clumped barbs. Crooked black teeth filled the ragged hole of his mouth.

Everything in the room spun around the screeching fiend.

The whirlwind tossed Katrina against the wall. She slumped to the floor in a heap.

Sasha collided with a flying chair and spun to the ground. She called to her fallen friend, but the roar of the wind beat back her voice. Flat on the floor, she dragged her body forward; the relentless wind beating back at her with debris.

Above it all the screeching din of the raging god prevailed.

Sasha gasped for breath. The air seemed to be sucked away before she could breathe in.

Katrina raised her head and looked around dizzily.

With her last strength, Sasha called to her.

Katrina rose, as if to walk. The wind took her immediately and sent her careening at her friend. They tumbled together crashing against innumerable objects in the maelstrom. They came to rest in a small eddy in the corner of the room.

"Looks like we've really done it this time," Sasha said.

Katrina struggled to catch her breath. Between gasps, she managed to get out, "…one last crazy idea."

She struggled to her feet and helped Sasha to her side. Cupping her hands around her mouth, she yelled with all the strength she could muster, "You're not a god! You're a wimpy rodent whose only talent is passing a lot of wind! A side show freak!"

Sasha gripped Katrina tightly, "Wha…"

The beast glared at them and let loose with a roar. The wind hit like a freight train, crashing them through the window frame and thirty feet into the yard.

They came to rest near an old maple tree. The earth rumbled beneath their feet like ground zero. The crack of a hundred thunder bolts burst through the air.

A tornado erupted from the building and leaped to the sky, where clouds furiously gathered around it. Debris shot out in all directions. Just in time, the friends pulled themselves behind the tree. When they dared to look out, the tornado was terrorizing the school's ball field and heading to the local trailer park.

Katrina whistled. "What do you suppose the god of nature has against trailer parks?"

Sasha brushed her disheveled hair from her face and stared at her wide-eyed friend, her rage building.

"Let's go check it out, you said. No one will ever know. It's for the good of the animals! It'll put our minds at ease."

"Well, how are we going to explain this?" Sasha pointed to the hole in the ground where the science building once stood.

Katrina stared at the mess of scrap wood and broken glass, and shrugged. A tuft of soiled white pulled itself from the wreckage and ambled towards Katrina.

"Mr. Whiskers!" she shouted.

"Of course it would survive. It's the mammal's cockroach."

"Well, let's go," Sasha said with a sigh. "No reason to hang around here."

"Guess not. Hey, you know I have a friend who runs a kennel. Maybe we could..."

"No! No! I have had enough of animals to last me for the rest of my life, thank you very much."

"But..."

"But nothing, the next thing you know we'll be finding out that the god of war is a dog."

The two walked away from the wreckage with Mr. Whiskers perched quietly upon Katrina's shoulder.

"Live to fight another day?" Katrina asked.

"Live to fight another day." Sasha responded.

Mr. Whiskers squeaked.

DIGITAL VOODOO

The foot-falls beat out a rhythm as the two girls ran on a trail along the river.

"A nice fall day and you've got me out here running!" Katrina called to her friend. "I thought I was the impulsive one?"

Sasha scowled back.

"I don't mind, you know. It's a lovely day and the Charles doesn't stink."

Sasha turned onto a path cutting through the park towards the city while her friend happened to look across the river. Katrina had to cut over the lawn to catch up.

"So, we're going this way, are we?" Katrina smiled.

After a minute, Katrina spoke up again. "You know, you don't have to keep blabbing on about it. We could run in silence for a while." Sasha responded by picking up the pace. The two sprinted out of the park and came to an abrupt stop before the deluge of cars racing down the road.

Sasha punched the crosswalk button and paced the sidewalk.

Katrina rested against the light pole and caught her breath. After a minute she said, "I suppose this is about her?"

Just then the light changed and Sasha darted across the road. Katrina sighed and followed. Two blocks later, Katrina caught up as Sasha ran into a pastry shop. She was ordering a chocolate croissant as Katrina stepped up beside her.

"And a chocolate milk," Katrina added.

Sasha stormed over to a corner table and sat facing a wall.

Katrina paid and joined her friend. "Now this is worth running for!" She took a big swig of the liquid chocolate. "How about we run to Ben and Jerry's next?"

Sasha spoke while staring at her pastry. "It's not fair."

"I hate things that are not fair!" Katrina responded, slamming her fist on the table.

Sasha looked up at her friend, "Why, because they're unfair?"

"I was thinking unjust, actually," she responded with a smile.

Sasha returned a faint smile.

"So what's up, girl?"

Sasha sighed. "You were right. It is about her." She took a big bite of the croissant.

"Give, give."

"OK, you know she's added all my classes, and sits behind me."

"Like a puppy dog following you around?"

"There is nothing cute about it. It's creepy. Two weeks ago she dyed her hair to match mine. I swear she has a spy who reports to her what I'm wearing in the morning so that she can match it."

"Imitation is the most sincere form of flattery."

"Yeah, and stalking is the most sincere form of affection?"

"It sounds like you're developing a twin. It's probably a phase she's going through."

"She claims her name is Sasha, and hangs with people I know when I'm not around."

"Alright, that's pretty far up there on the creepy scale."

"Yes, and last week she started dressing a bit sexier, a bit more cleavage, and tighter jeans, etcetera."

"Have you spoken to her?"

"I've tried, but she ignores me. Anyone else, she'll chat up like an old friend."

Katrina frowned.

"I yelled at her after history on Friday and people came to her defense. They told me to stop being a jerk."

"Now Sasha, people say that to everyone."

Sasha stared her friend in the eye and set her jaw. "You know Janice Thornton?"

Katrina thought for a moment. "Of course. She's a sweet girl. Took a year off to go on a Peace

Corps trip, didn't she?"

"That's the one. She went all postal on me; threatened to put a venomous snake in my bed if I harassed Sasha again.

"Sasha, Sasha!" she raised her voice. "I know that's not her real name."

Katrina sipped her drink and asked, "So what happened today?"

"While you were sleeping in, my dear roommate, I went down to the dining hall. She was holding court at our usual table. Sweet little Janice bumped past me to take the last seat. When I walked over no one looked up. I said hi to a couple of people and they ignored me. It was like I didn't exist. And then, that witch, looked at me for just a second and smirked.

"She's taken all my friends ..."

"Except for me," Katrina interrupted.

"Yes, except for you." Sasha reached over and squeezed her friend's hand.

Katrina finished her drink and slammed it on the table. "How about that Ben and Jerry's now?"

"Hi Sasha. Nice to see you." A male voice broke in.

They looked up into the beaming face of Chad Perkins. They shared two classes with him.

Sasha looked to Katrina and rolled her eyes.

Katrina responded, "Hello, Chad."

He looked towards her as if he hadn't realized she was there. "Oh, hi, Katrina."

He immediately looked back to Sasha. "So, um, there's a concert next Friday and I thought you might want to …"

Sasha cut him off. "Next Friday. Gee, sorry, nope I'm busy."

"Oh," he looked down. "Maybe some other time?"

She just shrugged.

"Oh, okay, I understand." Chad gave a little wave, turned and left.

"You're so mean," Katrina said.

"He's not taking the hint."

"Hello Katrina," a melodic voice said from behind Sasha.

"What is it, South station in here today?" Sasha said.

Katrina looked up to see a near perfect twin of her Sasha. She was wearing the same running shorts as the real Sasha and the same color top, although it was tighter. Katrina scowled at her. "What do you want?"

"Well," the Sasha clone said, "I'm having a party and thought you might want to come along. It's tonight about eight o'clock."

Katrina was about to turn her down when a thought occurred to her. "Can I bring a friend?"

The fake Sasha's face lit up in a bright Hollywood smile, "Sure, I'd love to meet your date. Who is he?"

Katrina smiled back. "It'll be a surprise."

"OK, then, I'll see you tonight. Bye."

Katrina waved.

"Not you, too," Sasha growled.

"What? - choose it over you? No way. What do you say? Want to go to a party with me?"

"No, no, no way. You're not dragging me to that impersonator's room. There is absolutely no way that you can get me to go too." Sasha folded her arms over her chest.

At seven thirty the two stood outside fake Sasha's door.

"I can't believe you talked me into this," Sasha said sourly. "Are you certain you can distract her?"

Katrina met Sasha's gaze with one corner of her mouth up in a mischievous grin.

"Oh, yeah, for a second I forgot who I was talking to."

Katrina knocked.

"Who is it?" came a sweet reply.

"Doesn't it just make you sick?" Sasha asked miming putting her finger down her throat.

"Katrina."

It took a few seconds before the response came. "Katrina, you're early."

"Yeah, that's me. Just thought I could lend a hand setting up."

There was a longer pause before the next response. Katrina was about to knock again when they heard, "Alright, I just need a minute."

After a moment the door swung open and a broad faced grin contracted to a pout at the sight of Sasha. The clone stood frozen for a moment.

"May I come in?" Katrina asked as if she were alone.

"Um," the clone paused.

Katrina could see the wheels turning. Before the clone came up with another mono-syllabic response, Katrina pushed past her, dragging Sasha in with her.

About midnight they stumbled back into their own room.

Sasha collapsed onto her bed. "Well, that was fun," she muttered through clenched teeth.

"Yes," Katrina spun about and dropped onto her own bed. "I think it was, actually."

"Fun for you, maybe. You weren't being jostled, bumped and stepped on by people who couldn't see you. And not even one apology. It's like I don't exist."

Sasha gazed at her friend who seemed entranced by her nail polish.

After a moment of silence Katrina looked. "I'm sorry, were you speaking to me?"

Sasha took up her pillow and beamed Katrina over the head.

"You know she has a picture of Chad?" Katrina said offhandedly.

"What? I didn't see any."

"That's because you didn't go through her

drawers while Dave was distracting everyone."

Sasha smiled briefly. "I guess he learned it's not a good idea to kiss someone else in front of his girlfriend."

"I wonder if they'll ever get back together?"

"She deserves better. But what about the picture?"

"I don't know. They were kids in the picture. It was taken at a beach. Maybe they're cousins or something?"

The next morning Sasha woke up to Katrina humming. She rolled over to see the back of Katrina as she worked on her hair.

"Bee-Hive today?" she asked with as much effort as she could drag out of her semi-conscious body.

Katrina continued humming.

Lying there for a few more minutes, Sasha decided she wouldn't get any more sleep and slowly got out of bed.

"You seem cheerful today. What's up?"

Katrina didn't respond.

Standing next to her friend, Sasha said, "Boo," and jabbed her in the ribs.

Katrina screamed and backed away holding her ribs. Her eyes darted wildly about the room, searching every corner, even the ceiling.

"What's up, Kat?" Sasha walked up to her friend. "Stop playing games."

Katrina suddenly stood up, crossed her arms,

and leaned back against the wall.

Sasha let out a sigh of relief. "For a second there I thought...."

"Alright," Katrina cut her off. "Be ye poltergeist, spirit, ghost or ghoul, you should be warned that my Sasha will be back soon and she's not the kind you want to be messing with."

Sasha grabbed her by the arms and shook, vigorously. "What are you talking about? I'm right here!"

Katrina reached out to grab onto anything to brace herself against the violent shaking. Her hands wrapped around Sasha's forearms. Then her eyes focused on Sasha.

"Sasha? What? Where did you come from?" And then with a smile, "How did you do that?"

"How did I do what?" Sasha turned panting. "I was here the whole time, you just couldn't see me."

Tapping her chin with her index finger, Katrina replied, "That doesn't seem likely does it?"

"Do you think? It's that other girl; she's taking over my life. One more day and you may not be able to see me again."

Sasha fell into her chair and laid her head on the desk.

"Come now, you shouldn't let a little thing like this get you down."

"A little thing," Sasha sneered.

"That's right you're not a quitter."

"Nope, not any more. What can I do? If you

want me just look for the white flag, it's the battle flag for us quitters."

"No, no," Katrina pulled Sasha up into a proper sitting position. "You are not a quitter."

Sasha rolled her eyes.

"Remember back in high school. Who was it that convinced the school nurse that we came down with potato famine and had to go home? And who was it that convinced the entire school that the president was going to visit and we all got out of afternoon classes. And who was it who locked the entire faculty in the guidance office?" Katrina blazed a glowing smile at Sasha.

"Those were all your ideas, Kat."

Her smile diminished a bit. "True, but you were the one who made them happen. We wouldn't have been able to do any of those things without your planning and execution."

"We wouldn't have been involved in any of them without your warped, twisted, deranged, fly by the seat of your pants insanity."

"It was fun, though, wasn't it?" Katrina beamed.

Sasha smiled back. "Okay, but how can I do anything if no one knows I exist?"

"If you ask me, it's a gift."

Sasha perked up. "Yeah, I'm like a ghost. No one can see me. I can be her personal poltergeist until we figure this out."

"What ya going to do first?"

"Well," Sasha paused in thought. "First, I'm going to gorge myself on breakfast."

Katrina sucked in her breath.

Sasha smiled back, "If no one can see me, what does it matter what I look like?"

Katrina's smile brightened again.

That day she tailed her clone from class to class. No one looked at her all day. It was all rather boring. She wondered how cops managed a stakeout. Then, in the early evening, just before sunset it happened. It started just as dry and boring as everything else.

"Hey," a female voice called.

The clone swung around almost striking Sasha with her elbow. "Hey," she called back.

A petite girl in a loose black dress came up and gave the clone a quick hug. They started walking together.

"We missed you at last month's DV meeting."

"Yeah, sorry. I've been tied up working on my final project."

The newcomer perked up. "Really! I haven't decided which lesson I'm going to do. I was thinking twelve or eighteen. What are you doing?"

"Lesson 88," the clone said dead-pan.

The newcomer froze in her tracks. After another step the clone stopped and looked back raising her eye brows.

"That's super-advanced," the newcomer said tentatively.

"I wanted to stretch myself."

The girls resumed walking. Sasha pulled up beside the newcomer to catch every word said.

The girls continued talking in hushed tones.

"Who's the victim?" the newcomer asked.

"Oh, just someone who thinks she's special."

"I hate people like that."

"Indeed," the clone intoned.

"How's it going?"

"Very well, except for her best friend. The bond is strong, hard to break. But it's coming along."

"Well, this is me," the newcomer said pointing to a building. "Kick-boxing in the basement. You should join us sometime."

"Maybe," the clone responded. They gave a brief wave and parted.

Once the clone was home for the night, Sasha went back to her room to search the internet. Katrina was asleep in her bed.

Sasha started with DV Lesson 88, but didn't find anything. After hours of searching, she was about to give up when she saw something in the corner of the search screen. She blinked several times to verify that it was actually there. It was DV Lesson 1 in just a slightly dimmer shade of white than the page. It wasn't in the search results, but in the corner.

Clicking on it brought up a black screen. There was nothing in the web address at the top of the page and nothing to click on. Nothing happened when she tried clicking randomly over the page.

Neither did typing every key on the keyboard.

She went back to search and tried other lesson numbers, each coming up the same. She noted that other words appeared in that space just before the lesson number. When she typed in "DV Lesson 88" it did just the same as the others. Try as she might, the words flashed too fast for her to make it out.

Sasha awoke with a start pulling her head up from her desk, Katrina's hand on her shoulder.

"That doesn't count pulling as an all-nighter you know," Katrina said.

Sasha rubbed her eyes. "It would have been a waste of an all-nighter as I didn't find anything."

"Nothing?" Katrina pointed to the screen, "It looks like you've found the great black screen."

Pressing the back button on her browser, she pointed to the lower right corner of the now white screen.

"DV Lesson 88," Katrina read out loud. "What's that mean?"

"I don't know but it has something to do with what is happening to me. Now watch it closely during the refresh."

"Did you see it?" she asked once the screen refreshed.

"What am I looking for, exactly?"

Sasha pointed to the suspect words. "There is something else that pops up in that space just before these words, but I haven't been able to catch it." She refreshed again.

"Yeah, I see," said Katrina as she ran to her dresser and pulled out her camera.

"What?" Sasha asked.

"Oh, come now. We record the screen refresh and play it back frame by frame."

Sasha perked up. "That's brilliant."

"Not really. I used the same technique to capture some great shots of Patrick Dempsey."

Sasha raised an eyebrow.

"I was just 15, give me a break."

Reviewing the frames they saw the words, Digital Voodoo.

Sasha crossed her arms. "Voodoo, really Voodoo? This is twenty-first century Boston. How do we get Voodoo here?"

"Salem witches," Katrina responded.

They looked at each other for a few seconds and shrugged.

"Okay, but how do we fight it?" Sasha asked. "When I click on it nothing happens. I've been at it most of the night."

"There is this shop on a back alley in Newburyport, called Granny's. I think I saw some voodoo stuff there."

Sasha squinted. "When did you go there?"

"Last month when you were sick."

"So, while I laid here on death's doorstep you were off having fun."

"Pretty much, except for the fun thing. Jenny wanted to try a raw vegan restaurant in one of those old mill buildings converted to a mini-mall. I tried a bit but ended up eating from the convenience store across the hall from them."

"Raw vegan?"

"Don't ask me. It's the sushi of PETA, I guess."

Sasha sighed. "What about the Voodoo shop?"

"It's not a Voodoo shop, per se, more of a macabre nick-knack hovel. You'll see when we get there."

They arrived at the alley a few hours later. On either side were the backs of shops. On the street-facing side were bright and inviting window displays. On this side they were plain concrete or brick. A couple of aged trees grew in the middle of the path shading the area and adding to the general gloom of the place.

"Okay," Sasha said, "This is kind of creepy."

"Well, they are not going to put a Voodoo shop in Harvard Square now, are they?"

"A macabre nick-knack hovel," Sasha corrected.

Katrina led the way to a set of stone stairs that led below ground level. At the bottom a door led into the basement of the building. Above the door a small, hand-painted sign read: Granny's.

"How did you find this place?" Sasha asked.

Katrina shrugged, "Lucky, I guess."

"And would that be good luck or bad luck?"

Sasha asked with a wink.

They were immediately struck, not by the jumbled mess of a store, but by the overpowering odor of spices, incense, and other unidentifiable smells.

Sasha gagged and coughed. Katrina smiled and took in a deep breath.

After a couple of minutes, Sasha got to the point that she could breathe the spice soup atmosphere of the store. The room occupied by the store was long and narrow like the inside of a school bus. Running down the center of the room were floor to ceiling display shelves. Between the shelves on the wall and the ones in the middle, they had to turn sideways to navigate between the overstuffed shrunken-head pillows and porcelain vampire teeth.

After half-an-hour of searching they returned to the front of the store empty-handed.

"I thought you said there were voodoo dolls here?"

"Hum," responded Katrina, "Well, they do have some pretty creepy dolls." She reached out and stroked a wind chime made of animal fangs.

"We'll see." Sasha stormed off to the counter. A large black woman who looked old enough to be a great grandmother sat flipping through a copy of a fashion magazine.

"Look, can you help us?" Sasha demanded.

The woman turned the page and continued her perusing.

Before she could yell at the relic, Katrina touched her on the shoulder. "Here, let me try, invisible girl."

Katrina cleared her throat.

The woman looked up in surprise. "Well child, you gave granny a bit of a start. You know I get so tied up in my reading that I'd miss an earthquake. What can granny do for you, child?"

Sasha groaned and turned away in disgust. Would she be ignored forever, moving as a ghost through the world?

She shook the thought from her head and looked around while Katrina chatted with granny. As she turned, she noticed a narrow doorway with a bead curtain leading into another room. An 'employees only' sign was hanging conspicuously on the wall by the door. Walking up, she pushed some beads aside and peered in. Piles of various shaped small boxes filled the room. In the middle of this mess, a girl, no older than herself, sat at a table. A pile of emptied boxes littered the floor around her feet.

The girl looked up as Sasha parted the curtain. Cocking her head to one side she stared directly into Sasha's eyes. The girl stood up and walked over, looking Sasha up and down.

Sasha felt she should move, back away, but she was transfixed by the pitch black eyes of the other girl.

Stopping less than a foot in front of Sasha the girl smiled. "You're supposed to be invisible." She turned and walked back to the table.

When the eye contact was broken Sasha felt as if she had been released.

"It's not a very good job. Cheap work."

"Tell that to everyone at school."

The girl shrugged. "The force can have a strong influence on the weak minded."

"You can see me." Sasha stormed into the room. "How come?"

"Granny sees much, knows even more."

Sasha shook her head. "You're granny? Then who?" she gestured with her thumb back towards the counter.

"Oh, that's Rachel. Plays the part well. Tourists love her."

"But, that doesn't explain how you can see me."

"Granny sees much..."

"And knows more. Yeah, I got the fortune cookie version earlier."

The young granny dropped her smile. "You, girl, are the victim of voodoo. Weak, cheap voodoo. Who have you ticked off?"

"Some girl at school is taking a digital voodoo course and I'm her big project."

"Digital Voodoo?" She spat on the floor. "Digital Voodoo is a charlatans' game. A trick of mirrors, sleight of hand to the true magic." As she spoke her voice grew louder and deeper, like she was speaking into a 50-gallon drum.

"I'll tell you what to do, girl. Do you have any social media accounts with your picture on it?"

"Well, duh."

Young granny shook her head. "People never understand the power of personal items. Change your picture. It doesn't matter to what as long as you're not in the picture."

"But how would..."

"Are you going to listen or talk? 'Cause if you want to talk, you can talk outside."

Sasha pouted.

"Right now. You change your picture; she'll have no more power over you. She can't do anything beyond what she's already done to you. Then you have to take your identity back from her. You do that and you'll be visible to the world again."

Sasha stared at her intently. Their gazes locked for what seemed like minutes. Finally young granny spoke.

"Okay, you can talk now."

"How do I take my identity back?"

"Easy way, you kill her."

Sasha pondered it for an instant. "And the hard way?"

Young granny smiled. "It's hard because no one can tell you. It's your life; you're the only one who can figure out how to get it back."

"But, I don't know."

"Then, as master Yoda would say, 'stuck like this, you are'."

"Why are you quoting Star Wars?"

"We take good analogies where we can get them. Now go. I'm too busy with the dead today to worry about the invisible."

Sasha grabbed Katrina and headed out.

"Bye, Granny!" Katrina called over her shoulder. Outside Katrina continued. "That was a nice grandma."

"Katrina, I have to take my life back. How can I do that?"

Spreading her arms wide, Katrina responded, "Go shopping."

Back at the dorm they sat facing each other.

"I figure to get my life back I have to want it more than her."

"Okay," Katrina shrugged.

"I really don't think that I can want it any more than I already do. Therefore we have to make her want it less."

Katrina thought for a moment and then a wicked grin bloomed on her face.

On the third night of sitting in the clone's room Sasha finally saw how to log into the digital voodoo site. Using Katrina's camera trick, she managed to capture the password.

"My, don't you look disheveled," Katrina greeted her the next morning.

"Yeah, but I got the goods," Sasha said with a weak smile. "And after a decade or so of sleep we'll get to it." Sasha fell on the bed and dozed off almost immediately.

She awoke in the early afternoon. Katrina was out. Taking out her laptop, she entered the site. Besides rather dark graphics the site seemed rather ordinary. A couple of hours later Katrina returned Sasha's broad smile.

"Hello, Cheshire," Katrina said.

"I've found something that should just be perfect. Look," she pointed to the PC, "gravitas, living a fuller life. This should strengthen my grip on my life, while we work on the other half."

"It's amazing how much they use social media. A voodoo doll is supposed to be a representation of a person. On These sites we each build our own representation."

"So, what's this gravitas?"

"To start, I just change my picture to my family. A strong bond to me and not her." She said the last word with a sneer. "I've also poked everyone I know. Each one that pokes back builds me up.

"And, of course, I have to link to their main site for the mojo."

Katrina smiled. "Someone's been busy."

"Indeed, and now for the fun stuff."

The friends headed out to look up the clone. They found her leaving the dining hall. As they approached they saw Chad creeping up on the clone from behind.

Sasha and Katrina stopped and watched. Immediately behind her, he reached over her head and covered her eyes. "Guess who?"

"Chad," she said with a smile as she turned and wrapped her arms around his neck. They hugged and kissed deeply.

Sasha reached over and closed Katrina's gaping mouth.

"She did this for Chad?" Katrina asked.

"Apparently."

They stood silent for a few seconds.

"Okay," Sasha said. "I know how to end this."

She stormed over and pushed them apart knocking the clone to the ground. Chad looked down dumbfounded. Sasha pulled him in close and planted one on his lips.

"No!" the clone shouted as she got to her feet. She lunged at the two but Katrina swung her around and held her at bay.

Chad seemed to be in shock standing with his hands out staring at the clone. Sasha struggled to turn his back away from the other her. Once she was out of sight he relaxed and closed his eyes. When he did, Sasha whispered, "Kiss me, Chad."

The clone, with tears running down her cheeks, turned to Katrina. "I can't watch. Please you must stop this. I've worked so long. Please, I'm begging you; please stop this before it's too late."

"Sasha was never interested in him. You could have just waited for him to take the hint."

She started sobbing and fell to the ground.

"He's Chad. I've loved him since we were kids but he never saw me as anything but a friend."

After what seemed like minutes of making out Sasha pulled away. Chad slowly opened his eyes and smiled.

"Sasha."

"Yes, Chad, it's me."

He reached to pull her back into his embrace but she stepped away.

"Chad, I'm sorry to break it to you this way, but I'm not interested in you."

"But, we just…"

"That was a goodbye kiss, Chad. I don't want to be mean, but if you continue to bother me I will report you to the campus police."

He looked as if he were about to cry.

"There are plenty of girls on campus that would love a guy like you. Give up on me and find one of them."

He started to speak but she cut him off by raising a hand.

She walked past him to the clone. "You have done enough, messed up my life, and forced me to break that nice guy's heart. I hope you flunk your DV class."

She glared up at Sasha. "You've ruined everything. I will get you for this no matter how long it takes."

"What do I care? You can fiddle around with that digital stuff while I've got resources in the real thing."

The clone got up and started to leave.

Katrina said, "Maybe you can start by comforting Chad."

In a few seconds both Chad and the clone were gone. "That's the first time I've seen you have a fight over a guy you didn't want," Katrina said.

"Hopefully my last."

"We only missed one thing."

"What's that?" Sasha tilted her head looking at her friend.

"While you were invisible we could have stolen a case of Ben and Jerry's."

"You know what's a shame?"

Katrina shrugged.

"He's a really good kisser."

They both laughed and headed arm and arm back to their dorm.

Deronium

"It's almost midnight!" Dean said, looking to his twin brother.

"I know," Ron responded, rubbing his forehead.

In the shadow of an academic building they watched as two girls walked on a path through campus.

"Are you certain that's her?" Dean slapped his brother's shoulder

"Yes, the blond is her. The other is a friend."

Dean smiled. "Looks like we get a chance to meet her. He turned and took a step into the darkness. "Come on, we'll cut them off on the other side."

Ron grabbed his arm. "We can't. A, we don't have time and B, we don't know what will happen."

Dean shrugged and cocked his head to one side. "Only one way to find out." He pulled away from his brother's grip and jogged away.

Ron watched the girls for a few seconds and then followed after his brother.

###

"I think we're being followed," Sasha said.

They had just passed an alley between buildings as they crossed the campus to their dorm.

"Looks like the night's not over yet," Katrina responded looking around.

"Kat," Sasha sighed, "being stalked isn't a dating opportunity."

"Not the best one, no. But they may just be shy."

"Watching girls from the shadows is not romantic, it's demented."

Katrina touched her friend's shoulder and they stopped in the glow of a streetlight. "You're telling me that Brad Jenkins wasn't demented?"

Sasha rolled her eyes. "No, but I was young and he was a hunk."

"See?" Katrina started walking again. "Hunk overrules creepy."

As they turned the next corner, two guys stood in their way.

"Hello," they said in near unison. Each had one hand up and moved it slowly from side to side in what might have been called a wave if it weren't so stiff.

They were of average height, a bit scrawny with short orange-blond hair. Their shirts were light blue and loose fitting while their black jeans were narrow legged down to the ankles.

"Good thing we're not the fashion police," Sasha whispered to her friend.

"That went out years ago and they're not doing it right even for then," Katrina responded.

Both of the guys stared intently at Katrina. After a few seconds Sasha moved in front of Katrina and returned a healthy glare. "Sorry guys, we don't date twins. Rule number fourteen."

The one on the left said, "Sorry, what?" and scrunched up his face.

Sasha arched an eyebrow.

"Oh, you don't understand," the other said. "We just want to ask a few questions."

"Yeah," the first one picked up again. "First, are you Katrina Remilard?" he asked looking past Sasha.

"Who wants to know?" Sasha spoke up before Katrina could respond.

The guys looked at each other for a moment. "Us, Dean and Ron Pillsbury," said Dean.

"You idiot," Ron threw his arms up. "No name, no data, we discussed this earlier."

"Still, person," Dean said and Ron folded his arms in response. "We have to gain some trust here."

Katrina stepped up beside her friend and they shared a look that said: 'Harmless.'

"Demented," Sasha whispered.

Katrina shrugged.

The guys turned to the girls again and Dean continued. "You are Katrina, aren't you?"

Dean smiled at her while the other rubbed his forehead.

"Why, yes," Katrina batted her eye lashes.

As she spoke a quiet chirping sound echoed off the buildings. It died as Ron slapped his wrist.

"Late for something?" Sasha asked.

Ron turned and grabbed Dean by the arm. "Come on!" When Dean didn't move Ron pulled insistently and added, "now!"

Dean stood still. "We have a couple of minutes." He returned his attention to Katrina.

"Did anything out of the ordinary happen to you today? Anything unexplained? Did you interact with any stranger?"

"Excluding now?" Sasha asked.

"Please?" Dean asked.

"Strange, huh?" Katrina rubbed her chin.

"We had a blind date where the frat-boys-in-waiting spent more time watching the game on the screens in the restaurant then they did on us. Play offs, schmay offs."

"Actually," Sasha said, "recently, that's been kind of usual."

"Oh, yeah, lots of guys are jerks," Katrina responded, tapping her chin.

Ron raised his voice, "We have to go now, Dean!"

"Anything at all?" Dean asked.

"This is the worst pickup line I think I've ever heard," Sasha said.

"You have to give them points for originality, though."

Sasha nodded.

Ron started backing up the path. "Come on Dean!"

Dean took a deep breath. "Please, tell us what's so special about today?"

The girls looked at each other and shrugged.

Ron ran up to Dean, jumped in front of him, and shoved him in the chest. "Now!" he yelled, "or I go without you!"

"Not so fast," came a deep voice from behind the brothers. Two men stepped from the darkness as if they came out of nowhere. Both wore dark cargo pants, gray shirts, and baseball caps without any logo.

One of them was tall and slim and the other average height and ripped.

Dean and Ron turned to the intruders and stared for a second.

"Okay, let's go," Dean said and the two started to run around the men.

The big men caught them before they had taken two strides.

"Wait a second," Katrina ran up. "Who are you, and what are you doing with our friends?"

"Friends?" Sasha muttered to Katrina.

"Let go!" Ron yelled. "We're in a hurry."

"Not any more," the taller man said. "You are about to learn that there are consequences to your joy riding."

Katrina looked up at the man holding Dean. "Kidnapping is a federal offense, you know?" She waved an accusing finger at him.

The man turned his head toward Katrina and smiled. "This is for your protection."

"They may not seem it, but these are dangerous criminals," the other man added.

"What are you, some kind of police? No uniforms, no badges?" Katrina asked.

"Actually, I'm agent Able and this is agent Baker," the taller one said.

Katrina put her hands on her hips. "Like those aren't made up."

Sasha added, "All right, let's see some ID."

Able switched his grip on Ron and flipped out a badge that said FBI.

Just then the chirping alarm sounded and Ron slapped his wrist again silencing it.

Dean kicked Baker in the shin and tried to

pull away, but all Baker did was grimace for an instant.

"Do that again and I'll have to hurt you," he said through gritted teeth.

"Please," Ron asked. "Let us go. It may already be too late."

"It is too late for..." Baker started to respond but at that instant both Able and Baker disappeared as if they had never been there.

Released from Baker's grip, Dean fell to the ground. Ron helped him up and they both sprinted off.

Sasha and Katrina were left to stare at each other.

"I wonder if that was the strange thing they wanted to know about?" Katrina asked.

Sasha folded her arms across her chest. "Do you think we're freak magnets or something?"

"Or something," Katrina responded and they continued on to their dorm.

"I mean it. Why do these strange things keep happening to us?"

"I just assume they happen to everyone."

###

They were about to go to bed an hour later when a knock came at the door.

Katrina opened to reveal Ron and Dean, sweaty, panting, and resting against the door frame.

"Sorry, guys." Sasha stepped up. "No guys in the room after midnight. Rule number eight."

Katrina raised an eyebrow towards her.

Sasha responded to the gesture. "Yes, we

wrote it down with the others. It's a real rule."

"I think it might be time for us to update the rules, don't you?"

Sasha raised an eyebrow back. "Not right at this moment."

"Please," Ron asked, "We don't have anyone else to turn to. Please help us."

"At least he's polite," Sasha said.

"You would notice that."

"Breeding is important. We should add that to the rules."

"Please," both Ron and Dean said.

Sasha stepped forward, blocking the doorway. "Aren't you wanted by the FBI?"

"Impossible," Ron said. "There is no way anyone could know we're here."

"What about Able and Baker?"

"We don't know, but we need help. We have no place to go."

"I fail to see where that is our problem." Sasha stood firm.

Dean looked past Sasha to Katrina. "Please, Grandma Kat, we're lost."

"Grandma Kat?" Sasha turned to her friend. "Is there something you want to tell me?"

With her attention diverted, the boys pushed past Sasha and entered the room.

"Hey," Sasha protested.

"Grandma Kat, we're from the future. We invented a time machine and came back to see..."

He was cut off by two large men entering the room.

"If it's going to be a party, I'll get the chips and dip," Katrina said.

Sasha turned on the men, but stopped short when she recognized them. "Able, Baker, what are you doing here?"

They stopped and stared at her. "How do you know us?" Able asked.

"We caught your vanishing act earlier." She looked to Katrina. "About, what?"

Katrina checked her watch. "A little over an hour ago."

"Do you suppose?" Able asked his partner.

They looked intently at each other for a few seconds. Baker squared his shoulders. "Finish the mission and figure out the details later."

Ron and Dean backed away from the agents, but with little space to maneuver they were quickly cornered. As soon as they laid their hands on the boys the agents disappeared again.

Ron and Dean shook and stared at where the men had been.

Sasha caught Katrina's gaze. "That's twice."

Dean recovered first. "Grandma Kat, we came back to see you on this date because we were told you saved the world today."

Ron jumped in, "Sure, tell her everything!

"How did I let you talk me into this? We should be back at our time accepting awards and professorships. But, no, you had to play time traveler!"

Dean smiled and pointed to Katrina. "And we found her."

Ron rubbed his forehead and muttered.

"So," Sasha said. "Why don't you hop into your machine and go back to where you came from?"

"Time machine?" Ron said. "Like something

we would bring with us? Time isn't some wibbly wobbly timey wimey stuff. It's more like a worm hole."

"It is a worm hole," Dean corrected.

Ron sighed. "Yes it is a worm hole, but not your standard, every-day, worm hole. The point is, there is a starting point and an ending point that are fixed. The starting point is in the future where the device is and it can only be controlled from there."

"We have to be in the future to open the worm hole to get back to the future." Dean added.

"Wibbly wobbly?" Katrina asked.

Dean grimaced. "He saw it on a t-shirt somewhere and fell in love with the phrase."

"So it isn't a flux capacitor?" Katrina asked.

The boys looked confused.

"You'd think they'd have more culture in the future." Sasha shrugged.

Ron shook his head and continued. "We set our return trip for midnight but those goons showed up and made us miss the window. Now we have no way to get back to the future."

"If they had vanished only a few seconds earlier we could have made it," Dean said. "We got there just as the opening closed. It's as if they timed it to make us miss the chance."

Sasha leaned against her desk. "So the only solution is to build a device here and use that."

Both boys seemed dejected. Ron spoke after a moment. "We can't. At the heart of the machine is the element Deronium. It hasn't been made yet."

"It can't be made yet," Dean continued. "The technology hasn't been developed. It is only stable at absolute zero and is created in something like the large hadron collider. It won't be developed for decades.

"Until then," Katrina said, "you can stay here."

Sasha added, "and by here we mean in Boston, not our dorm."

"But, they're family."

"Says them."

"Okay," Katrina looked to the boys. "Do you have any money?"

"We brought a few thousand dollars," Ron said.

"Really?" Katrina brightened.

"Is that a lot?" Dean asked.

Sasha stepped next to her friend. "It'll do for now."

Katrina turned towards her. "There's the hotel on Beacon street. That's close."

"Tomorrow we could head out to Granny's. Maybe she can help."

"You're buying this?" Katrina asked with mock surprise.

"Disappearing goons and grand-geeks? Why would I not?"

"What about Able and Baker? Who are they?" Sasha asked then turned to the boys.

Ron and Dean both shrugged. Dean responded, "Like we said, we've never seen those beefs before."

"Alright," Sasha said. "We'll burn that bridge when we come to it."

The next day they took the boys to Newburyport.

As they turned into an alley Dean said, "cool,

I like the creepy vibe."

The alley quickly opened up into a brick court yard that had seen better days.

"Wow, I really like it." Dean said.

"What are we doing here again?" Ron asked.

"We're visiting Granny," Sasha responded.

Ron wrinkled his brow in confusion. Sasha continued. "She's a unique individual who has helped us in other, shall we say, interesting situations."

As they walked deeper into the alley two men approached.

"Able, Baker," Sasha stepped up with a smile. "Good to see you again."

The men's brows wrinkled in unison.

Katrina took her place beside her friend between the goons and the boys. "Yeah, we missed you."

"However," Sasha added, "I like the gray look much better than the blue."

Katrina studied them for a second. "Black was the best." Sasha nodded in agreement.

"You must have us confused with someone else," Able responded as he closed the space between them.

Sasha folded her arms. "Nope, this is the third time we've met. Each time you grab these guys here and then, Poof." She pointed to Ron and Dean with her thumb.

Katrina nodded agreement. "Without the 'Poof' sound of course."

The men hesitated for a second.

The girls stepped aside. "Go ahead," Sasha said, "but don't say we didn't warn you."

The men stepped forward, each reaching for

one of the boys. As soon as they made contact they disappeared just as if they were never there.

"I like them," Katrina said, "they're consistent."

Inside, an elderly black woman sat at the counter reading a fashion magazine. Katrina ran up. "Hello, Granny!"

"Well hello, child. Haven't you been in here before?"

Sasha grabbed Katrina's arm and pulled her towards a side doorway filled with a bead curtain. "Hi Rachel," she called over her shoulder.

"Hey, girl," the attendant shot back with a standard Boston accent.

"Wait," Katrina said following along. "That's not Granny?"

They passed through the doorway with the boys in tow. Inside, a young black woman sat humming with her eyes closed in front of a candle.

"Now what?" Ron asked.

"Now you break Granny's concentration," Granny said with her eyes still closed. After a moment she sighed and looked at the group.

"I see you are visible now," she said to Sasha. "Did you kill her?"

"No," Sash blushed. "I was able to take care of it using less extreme measures."

"Extreme is in the eye of the beholder."

Granny stared at the boys for a few seconds. "Why are you always bringing your problems to me?"

Katrina piped up. "Don't you like problems?"

Granny laughed. "I like you," she said to Katrina and then addressed the group. "Problems can be interesting. But, the only problem here is in their heads." She pointed to the boys.

"But these guys," Sasha pointed with her thumb, "are from the future."

Granny folded her arms and shook her head at Sasha. "You think I don't know this?"

"How could you?" Katrina asked.

"Granny sees much and knows more."

"But..." Katrina started. Sasha cut her short with a stern look.

Granny pointed to the boys. "They are where and when they belong. No problem."

"We don't belong here," Ron said as he stepped forward. He whispered to Katrina. "What are we doing in this magic shop, anyway?"

Granny raised her voice. "Granny sees much, knows even more, and Granny is not deaf." She emphasized the word deaf. "You are here hoping I can help." She spread her arms out. "There is nothing I can do because you are where you belong. They just have to accept that."

Granny pointed beyond them. "Now, those two, they don't belong here."

They all turned around to see the goons approaching through the store.

"Granny?" Sasha asked.

"What do I look like, Dr. Who?"

"But," Sasha said, "if you can't help, no one can."

Granny smiled and patted Sasha's arm. "The force is strong in you. You'll figure something out. Now go, find your destiny someplace else."

"Still quoting Star Wars," Sasha said.

"Still good analogies. Learn to enjoy them, you must," Granny said with a wink.

"Now, Granny has much work and little time before the full moon rises" Granny started pushing them towards the doorway.

Sasha pulled out her cell phone and snapped a picture of Able and Baker as they met up in the store.

"Hey," Baker called. "No pictures." And they lunged forward.

Sasha pushed the boys forward to block the men and as soon as they made contact Able and Baker disappeared.

"Convenient, that," said Katrina.

"A bit annoying, though," Sash responded.

"What's going on?" Dean asked.

"I don't know, but we can discuss it while you buy us lunch."

At lunch and twice more as they walked along the river-side park, Able and Baker appeared and disappeared. Each time Sasha took a picture of them. Finally as they sat watching a sailboat glide past, Able and Baker approached from upstream.

Sasha and Katrina stood up. "Hi, Able," Sasha said.

"Hi Baker," Katrina waved and winked.

"I don't know who you think we are, but I'm Alpha and this is Beta."

The two girls looked at each other and shrugged.

"Look," Sasha said. "You keep appearing and touch them," she motioned to the boys, "and then disappear. We think it's time to stop this."

"You are mistaken," Beta said. "We have never met before"

"Now, if you'll excuse us, we have to talk with your friends."

"You say something like that every time," Katrina said. "Can't you come up with anything new?"

The men pressed forward.

Sasha held up her phone. "Can I take your picture?"

"No," Alpha responded sternly.

"That's what you said the last three times."

"Don't distract me, honey," Beta said.

"Honey!" Sasha roared.

Alpha threw a side-long glance at Beta and sighed. "He didn't mean anything by that."

At that moment they reached the girls. Sasha stomped on Beta's foot and as he reacted in pain she kneed him in the groin.

Alpha stepped over to his partner and Sasha snapped a picture. "I don't like this pair." She signaled to Dean and Ron, "Go touch them, boys. Send them away."

Ron and Dean stepped forward as commanded and as they touched Alpha and Beta the men vanished.

"Now what?" Dean asked.

"We wait for the next pair," Sasha responded.

"What are we going to do to them?" Katrina asked with a smile.

"That depends on how they treat women," Sasha responded with a determined glare.

Katrina leaned in to the boys and whispered, "don't mess with Auntie Sasha."

They both nodded, shuddered, and took a step back.

A few minutes later the next pair arrived and Sasha stormed up to them.

"All right, Able and Baker, I'm in no mood to fool around here. You want those guys? You won't get them. Why? Because you'll disappear as soon as you touch them. How do I know? Because it's been happening that same way for the past two days. Do you want proof? I have it here on my phone! Are you going to be smart and listen up, or should I have them send you to oblivion?"

The men looked to each other and seemed dumbfounded.

Sasha pulled up her phone and opened the photo from Granny's and held it so the men could see.

"This is from this morning. This is maybe the third time we met." She swiped to the next picture. "This is lunch."

"That's when you had longer hair," Katrina interjected. "It was a good look."

Baker rubbed his clean shaven head.

Sasha quickly scanned through the rest of the pictures. When they got to the last one Baker asked, "What happened here?"

Dean spoke up. "You were less than delicate."

Able let out a low whistle.

Baker asked, "Is this for real?"

"Yes," Katrina responded. "You were a real jerk and deserved the kick to the privates."

Able responded. "I think he means all the pictures. Have you really been encountering us for two days?"

"And each time you just vanish after touching us," Dean said holding up his hands for emphasis.

Baker looked at Able. "Code fourteen?"

"Maybe," he responded to Able and then approached the boys. "We need to ask you a few questions."

The boys sat down on a bench and the men stood in front of them. The girls leaned on the back of the bench.

Able started. "Who are you, and when did you come from?"

Ron responded. "Ron and Dean Billings from 2059, and we invented time travel. This is our first trip to try it out. And you prevented us from making the trip back."

Both Able and Baker stifled a laugh. "Sorry boys, professor Roy Harrimond developed time technology on the campus of BC in 2061."

"Harrimond!" Dean turned to Ron. "He's a hack! He couldn't even write his own text book. Every page had errors we had to correct for him."

Ron looked up to the two men. "Really, he's a complete dolt. We don't know how he managed to get a professorship."

"Probably blackmail," Katrina threw in.

Ron rubbed his forehead. "We deserve the credit. We did the work. This should have been instant tenure."

Able rubbed his chin. "Professor Harrimond is well respected. If you worked for him, you probably took a joy ride through one of his early time tunnels and got stuck here."

Dean stood up. "We are telling you, we created it."

Ron tugged on Dean's sleeve. "What if Harrimond found our device and claimed it as his own? Even now he's stealing the credit for our work.

It's not fair."

"He would," Dean sneered.

Able and Baker looked at each other for a moment. Finally Baker said, "doesn't seem likely, but we'll check it out and be back shortly."

The two men started walking away. Then they were walking back. They only disappeared for a blink of an eye, less than a second.

Able let out a low whistle. "It seems you actually are the creators of time travel." Able nodded to his partner and Baker continued.

"We are time agents. We keep people from messing with the time line."

"Great!" Ron said. "You can bring us back to our time. We can straighten out Harrimond."

Both Ron and Dean let out a sigh. Dean added, "Finally."

Able and Baker again looked at each other for a moment.

Able spoke. "Sorry, no can do. As you've seen, every time we try to take you out of this time it breaks the stream and the agency wasn't built so we were never there to come back in time to get you."

"You see, occasionally someone or ones are supposed to go back in the past. It's part of the time stream. If they are brought back to the future it wreaks havoc with the time line. It's extremely rare."

"And confusing," Katrina added.

Able nodded. "The most confusing thing we run into."

"You have no choice but to stay," Baker said to Ron and Dean. He pulled a package from an inside coat pocket. "To help out, however, we've brought this." He tossed it to the boys. "In it you'll find social security cards and other documentation to allow you to fit in here."

The men turned and vanished.

"I'm going to miss them," Katrina said.

Dean and Ron sat quietly for a few moments. Finally Dean spoke. "Looks like a do over. We can do anything here and now."

Ron scowled. "We need to get back to our time."

"You heard the time guys," Sasha said. "This is your time line now."

"Besides," Dean said, "there's no Deronium at this time."

Ron stood up and walked to the railing overlooking the water in thought. After a minute or so he turned around. "Then we have to focus our efforts on creating enough Deronium to build a device here."

Dean walked to him while speaking. "It will take some doing." He gestured to the world around him. "These are primitive times. It will take years."

"At least we have something to focus on," Ron said.

"Alright," Dean smiled and held out his hand.

"Done," Ron responded taking Deans hand. "And we'll put Harrimond in his place."

In the fall of 2046 Dean arranged to meet Ron and Katrina in Newburyport on a Saturday afternoon. Ron arrived first and walked along the river-side park enjoying the comfortable weather and watching the boats. An hour or so later Katrina showed up with two young children in tow. The red-headed twins burned up energy running around their grand mother.

Ron walked up to Katrina and she immediately embraced him. "It is so good to see you," she said with a bright smile.

The boys ran up and stared at Ron. Katrina knelt down. "Boys this is an old friend of mine." She patted one of the twins on the head. "His name is Ron too."

The young dean held up a throwing disk and asked, "Do you want to play?"

"Maybe later," Ron responded.

The boys ran off towards a man playing guitar with a ragged old dog lying beside him.

Ron looked to the young Ron and Dean and then to Katrina rubbing his forehead. "Why'd you bring them?"

"I'm watching them for the weekend, and they do so like it out here."

"There you are!" Dean's called from from a short distance down the walk.

Katrina waved and Ron looked down.

Dean came up with his wife June. They hugged Katrina in turn and exchanged pleasantries.

Shortly Dean turned serious. "I've asked you here to say good-by."

Ron and Katrina looked at each other and then back to the couple.

"You see," Dean continued, "Our son and his wife are expecting."

"That's great!" Katrina beamed as she took Deans hand. "Congratulations."

Ron forced a smile.

"I'm retiring and we're moving to Atlanta to be closer to them."

Katrina, still beaming, hugged both Dean and June. Ron repeated the gesture and tried to look happy.

After a moment of basking in everyone else's joy Ron asked Dean aside.

"So that's it then? You're not going to help me straighten out the time line?"

Dean patted Ron on the back. "You're still clinging to that, are you? Look, deronium is now developed. You don't need my help any more."

"But our plans?" Ron turned away. "We were going to straighten out the future and get the glory and fortune we deserved instead of letting Harrimond take it from us."

"Ron, I'm happy with my life here. This is my dream."

Ron didn't respond.

"Did you ever think that the reason the time agents couldn't bring us back is because if we controlled time travel that something terrible happens and the future would be ruined?"

"It's just not fair."

Dean slapped him on the back. "Give up on fair and search for joy instead. Rather than glory and recognition seek fun."

Once Dean and his wife left, Ron leaned on the railing overlooking the river and watched the birds. Someone tapped him on the shoulder. He turned to see two large, well dressed men.

"Remember us?" the bigger one asked

Ron squinted and looked closer.

"I'm Able and this is Baker."

"Didn't expect to see you again." Ron looked down.

Able moved beside Ron and pointed to Katrina and the boys. "You see them?"

Ron focused on the two red-haired children.

"They're going to grow up and create time travel."

Ron shrugged. "And then be ripped from their time and be trapped here. They'll be slaves of time. The only thing they'll get is having their names immortalized in the periodic table ."

"Yes. Nice that you got to name the element after Dean and yourself."

"I had always dreamed of more. Only a few geeks and historians will remember who we were and what we did."

Baker spoke up. "Dean made the best of it."
"So?"

Baker continued. "We have an offer for you."

Ron perked up. "Like what? You'll give me back my life?"

"That can't happen. But we could have something better," Baker smiled. "We're authorized to invite you to join the agency."

"Really?"

"Yes. But first you need to fill those little heads with visions of their grandmother's heroism, so they'll be properly inspired to build a time machine in the future."

Ron looked at his younger self. "Is this why I needed to stay in the past? To get the ball rolling?"

"That and develop Deronium. Which is what makes time travel possible," Baker said.

"I'll be an agent like you?"

"No," Able responded. "You may have some missions, but we really need you more on the technical end of things. There is still much about the equipment that no one truly understands."

"As you said, Harrimond is nearly useless," Baker added.

Ron smiled.

Able and Baker disappeared just as a tossed disk struck Ron in the side of the head. He leaned down and picked it up.

The younger him and Dean ran up. "We're sorry, Ron. Are you ready to play now?"

He knelt down and looked into their bright young eyes. "Sure, but first I must tell you the most amazing story about your grandmother."

"What about grandma Kat?" the young Dean asked.

"She once saved the world...."

THE SWAMI OF TIME

The floor looked like a dried up mud pit. At the end of the counter some kind of meat hung from a hook. The blue goo that dripped from it had formed a puddle on the counter. The smell, well, the smell wasn't good. All in all, not bad for a Latarian diner. The purple blob of a waitress could even spit out some English.

I had relied on the chaos principle to find the place. It was the first sight I saw after dragging myself out of the carcass of my ship.

My ship!

I'd picked up the remaining good pieces and put them in my pocket. The rest looked like a bomb went off in a sheet metal plant. The Hazmat team would arrive about the time the core meltdown consumed the rest.

I was due for a break. My cup had been overflowing with bum deals, rotten partners, and customers that just couldn't pay.

I was in no mood for it when the little whelp tugged on my jacket. I spun around. It had dropped to its knees, clasped its hands in front of its face and trembled, the universal sign for: "Hello, please don't hurt me." Usually I only got this sign after bashing someone in the mouth. I kicked at its head, missing by a hair or less, and flopped off the stool.

Big black eyes stared down at me from a big green head on top of a pint-sized body. An Icarian: nothing to be concerned with – a teething baby could take them in two out of three falls. It was still trembling, obviously thankful I had missed and hoping I wouldn't try again.

Don't get me wrong, I had nothing against the things, but they just had no backbone. Let anybody push them around and they'd say, "Thanks have a nice day." I just couldn't stand to be around something with that little self respect.

I regained my stool and turned my back on the thing, concentrating on my sandwich. It occurred to me that the squib would probably taste better, but I was too tired to clean and dress it.

"You will help me," it said.

I continued eating, wondering in the back of my mind if I could really digest the stuff.

"Ten o'clock," its voice turned shrill like a drowning song bird.

"Sorry, friend, but it's just nine forty. You're obviously on galactic self time."

"At ten o'clock you'll seek the rest room. Remember my words and live. You will do me a favor in return for this information."

"Sorry, squib, but I don't play party tricks, and

I owe you nothing." I swung around to kick it away, but it was already headed for the door with its big green ears flapping against its skull.

I didn't have a clue what the thing expected me to do, but my less-than-eloquent reaction had obviously squelched its plans. I watched it trudge off to find an easier mark.

I felt my stomach filling out. Yep, the stuff had started to set up, like cement.

After a while my body commanded my attention. Probably a side effect of actually getting food in my mouth. I stood up to head to the can. The image of the squib came to mind. I paused, wondering why I'd remember such an insignificant encounter. It didn't deserve the time, so I brushed the thought aside and started towards the commode, only to be blasted back in mid-stride.

Some time later I pulled myself from the rubble. A Jovian freighter had crashed, taking out half of the building and all of the restroom. If I had been just a bit closer, it would have been mutilation city. The squib obviously had something to do with it. I didn't believe in fortune telling squibs anymore than the tooth fairy. It had to be a setup. The squib used telepathy or mind control or something to maneuver me, and then went to all the trouble to crash a freighter.

No, the timing was too precise. No one could crash a ship to within a half meter at just the right instant. The ship had to be an illusion too. Whatever it was, the squib was the source.

I could put up with a lot. Heck, I was married twice. But, no little squib was going to play me the fool. I stormed out onto the street, looking for the wretched creature.

I fought my way through the crowd of onlookers. Directly across from the freighter impaled building, the holo-ad of a street vendor caught my eye. With an event like that it was doubtful he'd remember a little green squib.

"How come you're not over with the other spectators? You ain't from around here, are you?"

I shrugged.

"That's a Jovian freighter "

"Yeah, so what?"

"The Jovians ain't got no smarts. Never got past ballistic systems. They build them big and cheap. Don't put in no landing thrusters. Most of the time they wipe out the delivery site. Those who deal with them regular give their neighbor's address."

I opened my mouth to speak. "Okay, I have..."

"You're Jason Micheau, aren't you?"

"Look, nobody cuts me off, and how do you know my name?"

"One of them short green guys told me you'd be coming to me after the crash."

"Oh, really?"

"Told me to tell you he's at Singularity Center."

"Did it say anything else?"

"Yeah, in less than a year my wife will have twins."

"Great," I said, starting to plot the path to the center. It could have been a trap, so I had to take an unexpected route.

"The real hoot is that I'm not married!"

The fool was obviously in on it, or it was another mirage planted by the squib. I started off into the darkness. Down a couple of alleys, some side streets, and I was in an alley opening on the west of Singularity Center.

"Mr. Micheau." The squib stepped out from behind a box.

My gun was out before I could think. It was a miracle I hadn't blown the thing away out of reflex. It had one hand up and its eyes closed tight. The universal sign for: "I'm not going to like this!"

"Get out of my head squib!"

"I am not in your head, nor is this an illusion, drug induced or otherwise."

"Then what about the freighter, and how come you seem to know what I'm thinking?"

"In another time stream, you tell me."

"So you're a fortune teller."

"No, my tagrim, or spirit, travels the time streams. I can follow one to the end of the universe faster than you can draw your gun." It put its hand behind its back and rocked on its heels, like a kid. "In fact, my tagrim is split into pieces so that at any time

I'm following hundreds of time streams."

"That's nice," I said, stepping forward until the tip of my gun was against the little guy's green skull. "Let's say I don't believe you and pull the trigger, blasting your body into millions of tiny pieces."

"You won't." It put its fingers in its ears, the universal sign for, 'I'm not listening to you,' or 'there's something alive in my ears.' I forget which.

"You think I won't?"

"In this time stream you do not. It's a fact."

"Well here's a fact for you," I said, beginning to squeeze the trigger.

"Have you thought this through?"

"I've wasted too much thought on you."

"If I really am controlling a complex illusion in your brain, then how do you know that you're pointing the gun at me rather than yourself?"

I looked down into its stupid, doe eyes. The squib had a point, one I didn't like. "What if I just left you here?"

"Then how would you know when you're free from the illusion? If it is truly an illusion your only choice is to follow through and hope I release you at the end. If I know the future, then not only have I saved your life but I can be useful to have around. It is the latter, and as an added bonus, at the end of this you'll end up with a new ship. A ship that is far beyond what you could ever expect to own.

It held its hands out together as if offering an

invisible present and then bowed.

That eliminated the question: "What's in it for me? What's the target?"

"Genghis Sin, an Icarian."

"A rough name for an Icarian."

"He is unusual," its voice lowered to a hush.

"And where is this distinctive Icarian now?"

"I don't know."

"I thought you were clairvoyant or something?"

"I know the time streams of the future. I know not the past except what I experienced, and cannot see in the present anything but that which is around me. I do; however, know where he will be a moment from now."

"Let's assume, hypothetically, that I'm willing to help you. Why do you need me, oh great Swami of Time?"

"You are talented in physical ways that elude my race." It made a pathetic little muscle on its stick-like arm."I cannot get to him, we can."

"So, you want to waste this guy for what? Stealing your girl or dumping your mom?"

"No, he will not be hurt, at least not killed."

"Then what do you want him for?"

"It's an Icarian matter."

A secret not spoken is a secret kept. I let it pass. "Okay, I'll play along for a while, but if this turns out to be some kind of trick, I'll blow you away and figure out the details later."

Singularity Center was more than a klick wide at its base and rose some two thousand stories into the night sky. The squib led me through a hidden back entrance. Even though it was a public building, I felt better sneaking in. We marched right into the service elevator and up to floor fifteen-thirty-six.

"Is this it?"

"We will face the first challenge in the stairwell on our way to fifteen-thirty-seven." It wrung its arms together, like a braid, at least two full wraps.

"What are you made out of - jelly?"

"No," it said, very matter of factly.

We headed down a brightly lit hallway. It gleamed of wealth. I'd have to pawn everything I own to spend one night in their cheapest room. It was sick how the wealthy squandered their resources, although I'd like the chance to do some real squandering.

A thought occurred to me as we continued on our way. "The street vendor back at the crash-site. Is he really going to have twins?"

"He'll be so elated by the news that he'll stop off to celebrate tonight. He becomes extremely drunk and wakes up in the morning married. Not a bad marriage, but he'll never really be happy with her. The children will be his only joy."

"If it's that bad then why set him up like that."

"If I hadn't spoken to him he'd die in an accident in sixty one days, nine hours, and seventeen minutes."

"You're a chronometer too? Say! Tell me, who's going to win the inter planetary title next year."

It stopped and stared up at me through long narrow slits that could have been drawn on. "In every alternate time, no matter how different you appear, you've always asked that same question. In another stream it would bring you happiness. In this one it does not. You squander it and end up worse than before.

"Then in some alternate universe I'm living fat and happy."

"You misunderstand. There is only one reality. A moment from now or further into the future, decision and actions haven't happened. All possibilities exist until that point in time is reached, a decision point. Once there, only the action taken exists and the alternate actions and their time streams no longer exist."

"Yeah, right, some mumbo-jumbo."

We arrived at the stairs, a simple nondescript panel door set in the wall.

"As soon as we enter we'll be picked up by a roving monitor. It'll be at the top of the next landing. You must destroy it before it can lock on us, so fire as soon as the door opens. A random pulse fired at the upper landing will distract it. With time to aim, your next shot will obliterate it. Ready?"

It fell to its knees and stood up again. I didn't know what that sign meant. The problem with the universal signs was that no one understood them. I only knew a few basic ones. The first one I came across was: "Your hotel room is on fire." By the time I figured out what he was trying to say, everything in the room was in cinders. So far it was all babble. This would tell if the squib really had the sight. Of course I was convinced that it was mind control and I was still back at the diner.

I took the safety off my pulse pistol. "Open her up!"

The wild shot hit the underneath of the upper stairs. The sensor ports on the gray sphere rotated up. A clear shot. Blap! It was gone.

"Prediction number one worked out."

"Jason, they know something is wrong. We must hurry to the next floor. We will barely beat the investigating team," the squib said, scurrying up the stairs.

I grabbed it by the belt and hauled it up. The advantage of long legs. Setting up position, I waited. Just as the squib said, three men burst through the door. One, two, three, they went out. Not really knowing the guys, I hit them with a heavy stun. Their bodies tumbled down the stairs. They'd have some bruises, maybe a broken bone or two, but they would wake up.

"Switch to your dart gun," he said, one long finger pointing to my holster.

"I know where it is! Why do I need it? Are we going to be facing armor?"

"No, you're going to shoot someone through

a door."

"I'm starting to see where this future thing can come in handy."

"Hurry ," it said, pushing on my leg. "We have limited time."

I walked through the door to meet a flash of white. I dove, rolling against the opposite wall. Barely aiming, I fired at a figure. A second one rounded the corner down the hall. He went down quick. Then the squib walked out from the stairwell.

"Why didn't you tell me about them? Geez, they've got commando armor. What are you up to?" I leveled the gun, aiming at its right eye-ball.

"In the streams where I warned you, you were relaxed and just a bit too slow. You were vaporized. Come, we are almost there."

"Don't talk about my death in the past tense."

"In this stream yes, if a different decision had been made then you'd be just a pile of ash resting against that wall." Against my instincts, I followed the squib. We stopped after several course changes in front of room seven hundred sixteen.

"He is here. All you have to do is blow out the door."

"How do you propose that I..."

"The thermal device hidden in your boot."

"Hey, nobody..."

"Cuts you off, yes I know, but we must hurry. Reinforcements will be here soon."

"Why didn't..."

"Because there wasn't time."

"You ..."

"Yes I know what you're going to say. I've seen it and heard it, and it gets boring having to review it with people all the time. Please get the door. We're almost at the decision point."

The conversation had gotten too weird anyway. I pulled out the device, activated, and blew away the door.

Inside a squib lay by the open door of a high speed tube transport. Private by the look of it. The squib started to wrestle itself free of the debris. We came within three meters and stopped. This one had a different look. The scar from its right ear down to its mouth was the major reason. It was old and black, filling a spot where a strip of flesh had been torn from the face.

"What are you doing here?" the torn face demanded.

"Well, squib. I got you here. Now whatever business you have with The Face here better get done quick."

The squib closed in with its hand out.

The Face raised its voice. "Do you know who I am?" Its eyebrows jutted from its face. "I have friends who'll hunt you down. You'll suffer a slow agonizing death."

The squib touched The Face on the shoulder and they both dropped.

The last word the squib said was, "tag."

I bent down over them. They both appeared to be breathing, though The Face was twitching a lot.

"Mmm..." the squib was coming to.

"What happened?" I asked, when it seemed to be alert.

It stared at me for a moment, and then started dancing. I considered shooting it. Grabbing it by the arm I shook violently.

"You said there are reinforcements coming. What do we do next?"

"I haven't a clue."

"What? You're the Swami of Time, you swim the time lake or whatever."

"Not anymore, I'm free!"

I started to feel dark; another bum deal. "What do you mean?"

"I've given the curse to him."

"You mean that The Face here can see the future and you can't?"

"Yes, and it feels great!"

"The creature who just threatened me with prolonged torture will know where I am and what I'm doing, wherever I go?"

"Where you will be and what you will be doing."

"Who is this thing, anyway?"

"He's the Leader of the Cantre Syndicate."

My jaw dropped. "The Cantre Syndicate that controls the largest black market operation in the galaxy? The same organization that owns 17 whole planets? The one that support its own army? That Cantre Syndicate?"

"Yes, that would be the one."

"You stupid little squib, you've signed my death warrant."

"Don't let him bother you. It'll take a while for him to adjust to his new state."

"About how long would that be?"

"Hard to say."

"Take a stab at it."

"About two or three hundred years."

"I should pop it off just to be sure."

"No! You can't kill him."

"Look if it means my life I'll knock off whoever I have to!"

"What I mean is that he can't die. It's part of the curse. If you shoot him, the tagrim would return to him at the decision point and put him in a time stream where he doesn't die. The course of reality follows him now."

I kicked the twitching form. "If I can't kill it then, how can I escape?"

"No idea."

"Great."

"Yes, wonderful isn't it?"

Looking around, there wasn't much but the tube transport. I almost asked the squib where it led, but I couldn't stand another joyously ignorant response. I jumped in. The squib followed just as the door closed.

It was a real classy tube, no sensation of motion at all. At some cheap places they'd slam you against the wall on the corners. The only way to tell this was moving was by watching the countdown timer.

The squib's lips were poked out four or five centimeters and undulating. It looked like it was sucking on the end of a glass.

"Stop making faces!"

"When I'm happy I smile."

"That's not a smile, it's a hyperactive ringworm. Cut it out. Here take this," I handed him the pulse pistol.

"No! I cannot hurt anything. It is not in my tagrim."

"As you so gleefully pointed out, we don't know what's waiting for us. If you don't take it we may get killed."

"Oh, the times I longed for death!"

"Are you going to take it or not?"

"Not."

Great! We only had about ten seconds left. I took the pulse gun in my left hand and dart in the right and braced myself against the wall.

Swoosh, the door opened. A large open room lay beyond. I strained to hear any sounds of muffled words, feet moving, the rustle of clothing, weapons arming, there was nothing but my own heart-beat and the squib's breathing. I nudged it with my foot. "After you."

It looked up, its lips pulled back firmly into its face, "Me?"

"Run out as fast as you can. If there's anything waiting, you'll draw their fire. That'll give away their position and I'll blow them away."

"But I just got my life back."

"What about the 'how many times I've longed for death' thing? You could still take a gun and we'll go out together."

Its face smoothed out, eyes, mouth, and ears closed so that its head looked like a giant green egg. "Cut that out. The lip thing was bad enough."

After a moment its facial features emerged on its head again. "I will go."

I felt a twinge of pity for the squib. It had seen the future for who knows how long. Now it had to walk out into the unknown.

"I hope you've made your peace with the god of semi-firm, undulating matter," I nudged him with my foot again. "Get out there."

Tap, tap, tap; its little feet hit a rhythm echoing in the room. No gun fire, no sound of struggle, I edged out.

It wasn't a room, it was a hangar and what was in it brought a tear to my eyes. A Marauder-24, the most overloaded assault craft in the galaxy. I froze in place. It didn't have any registration markings. I quickly pulled out my transponder scanner. Nothing, it was a completely unregistered ship. It had to be used for smuggling, that's the only logical reason for stripping the transponder out. Finders-keepers was my favorite game.

Swoosh, the tube door closed. I didn't need the squib's power to tell me it was going back for another load.

The hangar control center was on an upper landing at the back. I bounded up the stairs. The minutes I had left were few and I didn't want to waste them. The hangar control was standard: release the lock and flip the lever, even a squib could do it.

All that was left was to get in the ship and seal it up before my company arrived. I'd be safe enough inside. No one with mere side arms would be foolish enough to attack a Marauder-24.

The squib had warmed up the engines by the time I made the bridge. "Good job, you little runt."

We left as the tube opened. A dozen or so figures stumbled out just in time to see me wave bye-bye.

I hadn't felt that good in a long time. I decided I'd do the squib a favor and drop it off anywhere in the galaxy it wanted to go.

"Where to, oh great Swami of Time?"

"No idea," it said, with its lips undulating.

Turtle in the Works

Underground was mercifully cooler. They had been inside, out of the surface heat, for over two days but Shecky continued to smolder. Maximilian Rogers, a man gifted in military arts by genes and training, was talking. His voice echoed through the tunnel, pounding on Shecky's ears.

"You realize, Shecky, that we could have been much more efficient in our search."

Shecky bit his lip. He had been baited into this argument too many times.

"Dart sensors," Maximilian continued. "A marauder 24 is equipped with cases of them. You know - just one of them could map this rat hole in less than a day. Locate the target. Then we cut a precision max2 laser hole, and fly right in. All done in under twelve hours, neat and simple. We've been at this for three days!"

"No!" Shecky blew up. "You've been at this for three days. Every moment of every day, even before we arrived on this junk hole of a planet. Listen, you muscle bound, burned out grunt. This is a covert mission. If the government or another corporation finds us out, we're sunk. Let me ask you, even with your pea pod brain, don't you think that a marauder 24 is a bit conspicuous? How could we explain it? 'My friends and I are taking the most overloaded assault craft in the galaxy for a little pleasure cruise.'"

"AAAHIII!" Jenny Tau came flying down the tunnel, shrieking like a banshee. Shecky looked up in time to see the dark figure bearing down on him. Before he could react, the genetically enhanced woman flattened him like a wafer.

She picked herself off the flailing toothpick of a man. Her head darted about like a bird on stimulants. Her body, especially her hands, constantly trembled. After spending most of her life in space, being on a planet was unnerving. The idea of megatons of planet above her head had decimated her personality. Now she was only good for trailing behind and screaming when something happened, or when it did not.

"You know," Maximilian mentioned to Gol Gol Tem Pal. "I could fix your girl friend. A little electrostatic pulse to the base of the skull. She'd be out for hours."

Tem Pal, average in most respects, brushed his hand through his stark white hair. "Would it hurt?" he asked.

"No. But if it's important to you, you could slap her up side the head a little."

A shout interrupted their conversation.

"Over here!" called Charles Richards. The old scientist was examining the dead end before them, his bushy beard wagging as he talked. Given the clothes, he would make a perfect Santa Claus. "It's definitely a manufactured wall, elliptical in shape, nine meters by twelve. The material is crystalline - possibly a liquid metal that has petrified. I wonder what held it in place: electro-magnetic adhesion, force field, or maybe capillary filaments..."

"Okay, Charles," Shecky interrupted. "What we want is probably on the other side. So, stop rambling and start examining."

Maximilian sprang to action. Grabbing Shecky by the collar, he yelled in his ear, "Even without a marauder 24 I can get through the barrier."

"All right," Shecky said, prying himself from the mercenary's grip.

Maximilian flung his pack to the walk. He began fishing through it like a toddler tearing through the wrapping on a birthday present. Shecky, looking on, wondered if Maximilian had spent his childhood locked in a closet.

Charles began twittering as he examined the wall. His constant noise making had always irritated Shecky, so he focused on Maximilian.

He was assembling what looked like a 6-foot sausage with a clustering of tumors about a foot back from the tip. A shoe box shaped thing was giving him trouble at the base. According to the label on the sausage, it was a hydrogen fusion force beam.

"Max," Shecky said. "Don't you think a fusion beam is a touch of overkill?"

"Nonsense, Shecky," Maximilian responded. "If you start with a low impact weapon and that fails, then you move to the next, and the next, and the next. You've wasted time and ammunition. The most effective course is to use the maximum amount of fire power that can achieve your objective, without obliterating it, of course. It has the added advantage of intimidating your opponent."

"Really? So, you feel this is the amount of force necessary to intimidate this particular wall into submission?"

"Oh, Yeah! We're going to make quite an impact."

A crashing sound pierced their eardrums like a box full of needles, which was driven by a sledge hammer wielded by Thor the thunder god himself. For a moment Jenny became her regular congenial self-assured person. The others writhed on the ground in agony. As the others recovered from the onslaught, Jenny drifted back into the private recesses of her mind, where she seemed to be meeting fictional characters from her childhood.

Shecky and Maximilian turned to see the wall crumbled to the ground. Charles stood beside the rubble, holding his walking stick.

"What have you done?" Shecky asked.

"The crystalline structure was not stable," Charles responded. "I applied a decisive force with my walking stick."

"Let me see that!" Shecky demanded, holding out his hand for the staff. Shecky hefted it, turning it over in his hands, feeling the weight. He caught Maximilian's attention and said, "This wall seems easily intimidated."

Maximilian slumped down beside the hydrogen fusion force beam gazing at it, forlorn, he caressed the smooth knobs of the tumors. He gave it a gentle kiss and whispered, "Don't worry baby, daddy will get you into action."

Beyond the wall they found a large chamber. Walkways separated squares of machinery on multiple levels. It looked like a three tiered chess set with deformed pieces. Shecky felt as though he was at an art exhibition entitled 'A Cataclysm in Metal.' Gazing past the machinery there were side rooms along the walls.

They entered and spread out. Jenny lay on the floor near the entrance, in a fetal position, rocking herself and humming "Twinkle, Twinkle Little Star." They were all quite relieved. Tem Pal mumbled, "I didn't know Jenny could sing."

Maximilian came upon a wall switch and instinctively ripped out his sidearm. The sound alerted the others and they dove for cover, except Jenny, who was now on to "Mary Had a Little Lamb."

Shecky, peering from his hiding place, called to Maximilian, "What is it?"

"Wall switch," he responded, poised like a

snake ready to strike.

There was silence for a moment as they took in the implications of his statement, then another moment as they realized there were no implications to his statement.

Tem Pal was the first to respond. "What? Were you traumatized by a wall switch when you were a baby? It's just a switch! This room is full of switches. Switches, buttons, levers, and probably even knobs!"

Maximilian crouched lower and tensed his body as he assessed the room. His neck muscles began to ripple, not a common sight on humans. "It's a trap," he said, and backed up against the wall to assure that nothing could sneak up behind him.

Shecky saw him backing up and realized, with the others, that he was backing directly towards the switch. "No! Max! The switch!" they shouted at the top of their collective lungs.

"Good! You understand," Maximilian said. "They're temptations placed before you, a trap saying, 'It's okay, press me, I want to be pressed! I'm your friend. Then they blow up in your face!"

As Maximilian's back hit the wall, a click echoed through the hall. Maximilian dove for cover with the others, but it was too late. Before he could reach safety, the lights came on.

Shecky sent Maximilian to guard the door while they explored. A rumble from the entrance stopped the group in their tracks. Jenny was up and walking towards Tem Pal calmly. Her expression was one you might expect to see on a clock maker's face after he had spent three years locked in his shop with only Jimminy Cricket for company.

Trying to remain at a safe distance, he ventured a tentative, "Hi."

To everyone's surprise she responded in a normal tone, "Uncover your ears." Gazing about the chamber as if considering something important, she added, "This is an unusual ship."

"Yes," he said, taking his hands from his ears. Usually he was a good conversationalist, but he seemed stuck in a one syllable rut.

"I wonder where the control room is."

"Well, Jenny, dear," he stammered a bit. "You remember, um, dear. We are looking for alien technology to save Shecky's and my company. Well we found this, um, alien ship and now we're looking for a, um, trinket that will give us the key to their technology before anyone else finds out."

"I remember." Her gaze was blank and unfocused. "But not how we got on board."

"That's okay, Love. Could you help search, though? You are a great pilot and a gifted technician. You can probably spot something of interest." This was true but Tem Pal's real intention was more likely to keep her busy in hopes of avoiding further breakdowns.

In one of the side rooms, Shecky found it, resting about 2 meters off the floor. It was a half dome about the size of a dog most sane people would avoid. Perfectly smooth and orange-green, it would have been tacky in any setting, like pink flamingo lawn ornaments which always seem to roost next door to the person who hates them the most.

Shecky called the others to join him.

Charles's power meter went off the scale. "Charles, what do you think it is?" Shecky asked.

"Well, on first blush, I'd guess either a portable power source or a doomsday weapon."

"Wow," Tem Pal said. "I vote for power supply."

"Why do you think that?" Charles asked with furrowed brow.

"Because, if it's a weapon, we're in deep trouble."

Jenny seemed oblivious to their conversation. Her expression was now one of a person raised by wolves trying to comprehend the difference between salad forks and dinner forks.

"Well?" Shecky asked Charles.

Charles approached the turtle device, his arm stretched out, fingers trembling. He slowed as contact became imminent. Shecky, knuckles white and neck strained, looked on. At last Charles's fingers came to rest upon the device. He turned to Shecky and opened his mouth to speak but was cut short.

The thing dropped to the floor, darted out of the room, and lodged itself under the first machine it came to.

General bedlam reigned for a few moments as the surprised group chased after it. "There it is!" "Get it!" "To the flight deck!" The last one was from Jenny.

Despite the threat of switches Maximilian raced to the aid of his comrades. He found them loitering about a large machine and called for a status report.

"What are you doing here? Didn't I tell you to wait at the entrance?" Shecky said to Maximilian.

"I thought you might need my help."

"Well, we don't. We found what we were looking for but now it's hiding under this machine."

"If we had the Marauder 24 we could simply lift this machine off, zap it with a tractor beam and haul it away."

"Look, I'm tired of hearing about that stupid Marauder 24. We don't have one, and we're not getting one, so get used to the idea!"

A recognizable sound emanated from under the machine. They crouched down on all fours like a pack of dogs and peered into the darkness. The glow of the device made it discernible.

In a clear voice it said: "You cannot detect me, my sensors are deactivated." It sounded pleased with itself.

Shecky was beside himself with anger. "We come all this way, risk death and imprisonment, and for what? A retarded alien power supply." He stormed off, kicking the machinery and cursing.

Tem Pal led Jenny away, trying to convince

her they were not inside a giant toaster oven. Charles and Maximilian remained, watching the device.

Shecky's ranting fit ended a short distance away. He flopped down on a machine, daring the universe to strike him again.

"What is it?" asked Maximilian.

"It seems to be a limited-intelligence power supply. There is, however, a very slim chance that it's a planet vaporizing bomb. Watch the thing for a minute while I get my equipment."

As Maximilian sat alone the thing peeked out.

His sidearm point blank on the device, Maximilian said, "Don't move," with authority he obviously felt.

The device made a quick dodge to the left. Maximilian's shot missed. The turtle thing bumped his foot, and said, "You're it," before speeding down the aisle. Maximilian rolled prone, targeted and fired again. Sparks flew as the energy pellet discharged on the surface of the thing. For a moment silence prevailed and smoke enveloped the alien device. Just as Maximilian was starting to relax the thing shot out of the cloud, heading straight at him.

Faced with the thing's shielding, the brave mercenary ran away.

Shecky closed his gaping mouth as he watched Maximilian try to stop the thing. Maximilian pulled a plasma bomb from his utility vest. The blast sent machinery reeling in all directions, but did not dissuade the beast on his trail. Next he tried flash grenades, used to overload sensors, then smokers, a blinding tactic. Other forms of explosives were pulled out in a dizzying array, each with great destructive success on the surrounding equipment. The turtle device, however, remained unscathed.

From Shecky's perspective the mercenary had gone to that magic land that all professional warriors actually live in, running to and fro destroying everything in sight with loud and violent glee. It was better to keep a safe distance, preferably back at the entrance. Blow it up and seal the fool in.

Maximilian activated his communicator and yelled, "Get out! Abort! Retreat! Run away! Whatever terms you civilians use for, 'run for your lives.' Our only hope is to get back to the tunnel and seal the entrance. I'll buy you time to get out."

Jenny and Tem Pal were the first out, followed closely by Charles. Jenny enjoyed the fireworks. The alien machinery and any knowledge it held therein was reduced to burning junk. They restrained Shecky from sealing Maximilian in.

After a few moments, Maximilian burst through the entrance. He grabbed the hydrogen fusion force beam and blasted the entrance. The others, already at a safe distance, covered up and waited for the crushing rumble to end.

In the quiet darkness again Jenny said, "No stars? How interesting."

Tem Pal had spent his reserves of patience convincing her that they were on a ship that looked like a toaster oven, fought to keep the illusion alive. "We're in the hold and the power systems failed. We'll be out soon."

Light exploded into the corridor. Shielding their eyes, they could make out the turtle thing as it broke free of the rubble. It dashed over to Maximilian, brushed his leg, and said, "You're it," and fled out of sight.

Maximilian lowered his head. His normally tense body went slack. "I give up," he said in frustration.

It emerged from the darkness and settled down at his feet. A swift kick flung it to the other side of the tunnel, back into the shadows.

Two and half days later they emerged from the planetary catacombs; the rays from the late afternoon sun bathed them in the surface heat. Jenny froze in stark horror. After a few minutes of prodding they gave up and decided to come back for her later.

"Think she'll need therapy when we get back?" Shecky asked Tem Pal.

"No. Put her in a space suit, tether her outside for a couple of weeks and she'll be fine."

"AAAHIII!" Jenny Tau came flying after them, shrieking like a banshee. Shecky looked up to see the dark figure bearing down on him. He had time to say, "Not again," before he was flattened like a wafer.

While freeing Shecky, they all noticed a whining sound that grew louder; a movement drew their attention to the west. A ship was approaching, and not just any ship. It was standard size for a crew of about a dozen, and of an unremarkable design. What really struck Shecky were the mountings on it, missile pods, torpedo doors, high energy beam weapons, and cannons covered it like leaves on a tree.

"What's that?" he mumbled.

"A Marauder 24," responded Maximilian in a dejected voice. "Now you see why we needed one."

Shecky had to admit that this was the Swiss army utility device of fighter craft, all the utilities you could possibly need plus twice as many that you could not.

A voice boomed out of the obscenely overdressed fighter. "Okay, Shecky, I'll take possession of that alien device now."

Shecky recognized it as the voice of Ivan Ricovic, son and heir to Galactic Prime Corporation. They must have followed and waited. They could have the retarded device as far as he was concerned, but he'd rot before giving in to this rival.

Tem Pal shouted, "And what will you do with us?"

"Why, maroon you of course. In a millennium or two someone may stray into this forsaken solar system and discover a flourishing civilization. But then again, considering the breeding stock I doubt it would make it to the stone age."

Shecky and Tem Pal fervently tried to talk their way out of the situation. They still had the bargaining chip of the turtle. Ricovic had no idea of the uselessness of the discovery. It would probably destroy the Marauder 24, once aboard.

During their efforts the turtle moved over to Charles and spoke. "The ship intends to do harm to Maximilian?"

"That is a fair assessment," Charles responded.

"Maximilian wants the ship. Is it acceptable?"

"It would undoubtedly be best for all of us if he did."

The group was consumed by light. Shecky wondered if the afterlife would be as nice as people said it was.

The light faded, replaced by an engulfing darkness. Blinking lights were the first to appear, followed by displays, stations, and chairs. The afterlife looked much like the bridge of a space ship. Maximilian started dancing and singing. Despite his physical training, he was a horrible dancer. "Maximilian, what are you doing?" Tem Pal asked.

"It's a Marauder 24. Look at the weapon control stations." Along two walls were bank after bank of targeting and launch systems.

While this exchange was going on, Jenny had fully recovered herself and had taken the pilot station. "Gentlemen!" she shouted. "I don't know how, but we are on the same ship that was threatening us."

"Where is the crew?" Shecky asked.

Maximilian drew his side arm and checked the

doorway to the rest of the ship.

Tem Pal went to Jenny. "You recover quickly, dear."

"Thanks, Hon. The sensors say that we're the only ones aboard. The previous crew is on the planet."

The turtle sought out Charles Richards and asked, "Did I do well?"

"Yes, you did exactly right. Now go play with Maximilian and don't let him hurt himself."

It sped off after Maximilian. Charles called the others together. "Listen. This thing is fabulous. It did a matter transference to get us here and get the crew off."

The others were dubious. "Based on the limited intelligence shown by the turtle thus far, it's inconceivable that any sentient race would give it command of that type of power to use on its own," Shecky argued.

"The turtle was designed to be a companion to a child," Charles countered, "to play with, protect, and probably even teach. To do so it must be something a child can relate to. It evaluated our group and determined that Maximilian was the child it was supposed to bond with."

"Inside, it is great technology for us, including a power source that can last for thousands of years and achieve matter transference. These features alone make it the greatest discovery in centuries. Heck, it can probably even teach us how the technology works."

"What about them?" asked Jenny, indicating the crew on the planet.

"Maroon them," came Shecky's response. Both Tem Pal and Jenny gazed at him with contempt. "Okay," he added, "just leave them until we can cover our tracks. We can't let anyone prove we actually made this discovery. It will have to remain an underground turtle."

Two years later, Indicorp had become the fastest growing corporation in the galaxy. Competitive companies tried to copy their technology, but by the time they had a product ready for market, Indicorp jumped to even more advanced technology, always remaining one step ahead.

Serious Stories:

These stories are serious in nature. They are not horror by any stretch of the imagination but deal with the difficulties humans have interacting with each other.

The Wish Maker's Magic Box

"Mama, Mama!" Pedro called as his feet beat up red dust from the dirt road. He sprinted through the marketplace, past empty stalls and closed doors. His voice was the only sound above the wind. The door, the only open door was in sight. He leaped up the stairs and into the doorway. "Mama, It's here! Come quick."

Mama paused her weaving, her gentle rocking slowed a bit. "Come inside and help your mother. There is much to do. Just think, if I ran off for every little curiosity no work would ever get done, and how would we eat then?"

Pedro dashed to her side and took her hand. At thirteen he had surpassed his mother's slight frame. Now at fourteen, he was a full head taller. Her hair flowed black down her shoulders. Wrinkles had just started to appear on her smooth skin, and added to the smile lines permanently etched around her full mouth.

She had been the favorite of the children. His friends had begged to come over to his house on story night. She used to play games with the little ones and had a smile, a song, or a shoulder for any who needed it. Pedro remembered all these things. Her skin had grown pale. He had tried many times to take her out in the sunshine, but she remained holed up in the shop.

He chanced to glimpse towards her eyes and he recoiled. Standing up, he stepped away.

"Mama, it comes from up river and the Sages are afraid of it. It must be real."

She settled in her rocker and began weaving. The practiced hands flitted from reed to reed like a pair of small birds fretting about their nest. The squeaking of the rocking chair added a melody to the work that made it seem a dance. Mama Gutierez was the best weaver on the river, they said.

"I was at lesson when Toma said that he heard that it has ruined the upriver Sages. He wants to destroy it, if he can. You deserve this!"

"If the Sages want to destroy it, then it must be evil. I've had my fill of it." Her voice was solid and strong. She would not be moved. Pedro rubbed his hands together. The sweat made them slick. He turned, not wanting to see her reaction to his next words.

Timothy O. Goyette

He started once, but only a peep came out. He started again. "Mama. The witch is with them. The Sages are working with her."

The squeak-squeak of her rocker stopped. He had promised himself never to mention the witch in his mother's presence. His heart thundered in his ears as the silence built.

The rocker started again. Pedro walked tentatively to her side. "I'm sorry! But it has to be real." He forced himself to look directly at her face, the sunken eyelids which had been sewn shut, covered the empty sockets. The lids seemed unnaturally dark as if light was taken away with the eyes. "You can have your eyes back."

"I filled your head with too many stories when you were younger. Pedro, it's real to you because you are young and you want it to be. What down-river foolishness. A magic box isn't going to grow eyes back. Now, go prepare a frame. The Diegos have ordered ten chairs, and we can use the extra money."

He raised his voice. "No, Mama! Come with me now." She stopped her work, folding her arms.

He waited for only a moment. Grabbing her hands, he pulled her from the chair. Her weaving tumbled to the floor.

"I will not become a spectacle, trotted out before my neighbors to be gawked at. I settled with it long ago and that's the end."

Pedro pulled harder. "I'm still your mother!"

He strained against her arms. She remained

rooted in place. He had never won tug of war against her, but this time he had to. He grunted with effort, yanking her forward. Each step towards the door became easier.

"This is for you," Pedro said dragging her out on to the street.

As the sun hit her face she stopped struggling, with a sigh. She turned her face so that her features were awash in the golden hues of the sun. "What time is it?" she asked.

"Nearly sunset."

"What color is the sky?"

"It is pale blue, almost green. The clouds are touched with red."

"Then tomorrow will be another dry day."

"I'm afraid so. We had better get moving Mama."

The woman bent her head, letting her hair cover the sides of her face, and held her elbow out for her son. He took her arm gently and guided her down the road. They walked past the wooden buildings that made up the market. Each was brightly painted and bore a symbol for the items being traded there. Each roof was thatched with wide leafed water plants. Pedro's first job, as with most children, was collecting these plants.

They rounded the corner to the buzzing sounds of insects. A living curtain lay ahead between them and the river. Each was about the size of Pedro's little finger and had bright silver wings. The veil of lillywan flies parted at their presence. The Sages had set them there to keep the river insects out of the village.

"I hear someone," Mama said as they approached the back of the assembled villagers.

"We're almost there. The whole village is gathered around a buckboard wagon. There are torches on each corner. The Wish-maker is on it. There is something beside him, it must be his magic box."

"Have they started? Is it real?"

"I don't know, Mama. It's hard to tell."

"Let's wait here until we find out."

A lump rose in his throat. "Okay." They stood a few paces behind the gathering, in the shadow of the tall Willow tree.

The crowd massed about the makeshift stage. The torch light cast an orange hue about the Wish-maker.

"What does it look like?"

"It doesn't look like any kind of box. More like a large, soft stone that has been shaped by the wind. It has many round parts to it, and is the most unnatural gray color, with scratches of red and yellow."

The Wish-maker pranced up and down the flatbed. "Gather around friends! See the amazing magic box!"

To one man he called,"Boots that never wear out!" To a lady in back. "Good Lady, have a full line of cookware!" To a bearded man in a leather jacket, "A superior knife! All of these, and more! Arrows of perfect balance with an ever sharp point!" He squatted down and leaned forward as if sharing a secret. "Seeds for ever-bearing fruit trees."

A murmur ran through the crowd.

Jumping to his feet he caught the eye of a young man with a woman at his side. "An ever-blooming rose for your sweetheart, to show your undying love."

The couple colored in embarrassment as the mass of people took to laughter.

"Who will be first?"

Voices shot out from all parts of the throng, each suggesting a friend or relative.

"The fee is a five weight of silver, but for the first it will be just a single weight! Come now, who will it be?"

Pedro stepped forward only to be stopped by a tug on his arm. He turned ready to pull Mama forward.

"Please, Pedro, let's wait. Let someone else be first. If it's a fake then we can just go home." Her shoulders were hunched over more than usual.

"Okay, Mama."

"I'll try it," came the voices of many.

A group of men approached along the river bank. Pedro recognized the Sages by their short cropped hair and fine trimmed beards. Toma was at their head.

"Stop this heresy!" Toma called out.

"Good sir," the Wish-maker responded. "Perhaps you would like a wish?" Then he called to the audience. "Cheer on our wisher."

The roaring calls became so great that Toma's words were drowned out.

"Mama, we have to get you to the magic box before Toma ruins it."

As he started to lead, Mama pulled back. "Are you sure, Pedro?"

He took her hand. It was cold and trembling, though the night was warm. She sniffed as if covering a tear that could not come. "No," he responded in a whisper.

They were greeted as they reached the crowd. "Good evening Mama Gutierez."

"Pardon me, Mama."

"It is good to see you out, Mama."

The villagers made way for them so that a path opened directly to the wagon. A hush fell over the throng so that the sounds of crickets and frogs could be heard. Mama Gutierez kept her head down, her hair hiding her face, and mumbled greetings back.

The Wish-maker seemed speechless, but Toma was not. From the back Pedro could see the sage's hands waving as he yelled at the outsider. "You have no business selling your junk to these hard-working men and women. We've heard how you have been run out of town after town, taking families' life savings with you. By the waters, we won't let you steal from this village, you down-river trash!"

Toma only noticed them when they were just behind him. "Mama Gutierez, what are you doing here?" he asked quietly.

Pedro answered, "I've brought her to make a wish."

Toma seemed to pause in thought for an instant, then his eyes widened. "You foolish, foolish boy." He latched on to Pedro's arm and shook. "You got Mama's hope up for this river slime. Do you know what you've done?"

Turning to Mama, Toma touched her gently on the shoulder. "Go home now. Get away from this and try to forget, again."

Hector, a big bearded man stepped up and slapped Toma's hand away, "Let her wish."

"Yes, give Mama her wish," called another voice from the crowd. Soon a great chorus of voices swelled into the night all calling for Mama's wish.

Hector climbed onto the wagon. "I'll pay her way," he called, dumping a five weight at the feet of the Wish-maker Soon others were throwing coins and precious metals onto the wagon. The Wish-maker was yelling, but even in the front Pedro couldn't hear him over the commotion.

Where was Mama? He turned but she wasn't there. He looked around, pushing people aside, looking in one direction then another. After what seemed minutes he saw four men lifting her onto the wagon. He scurried up after her. Cheering and applause erupted from the crowd. The Wish-maker stammered and mumbled.

Hector took the Wish-maker by the collar. Lording over him the big man said, "Eight years ago a plague took our village. We all lost family. Only the witch could save the village. But she had a price. Mama Gutierez paid with her eyes. You're going to give her the wish or you'll never leave this stage."

The Wish-maker looked closely at Mama for the first time. He reached over, moving her hair aside, then jumped back with a gasp. "But I can't...that's not how it works..."

Pedro called out, "I wish for my mother to see!"

After an outburst of approval the villagers drew quiet. Everyone was focused on the magic box. Minutes passed with no sign of activity from the magic box.

"It can't do miracles," the Wish-maker called. "It's only good for tools, trinkets, and things like that. You can't expect it to..."

"Shut up," Hector growled.

More minutes passed.

"I think it's a fake," someone near the front said. More murmuring came from the crowd. Hector pulled the Wish-maker closer.

Rattle.

The magic box began to shake. Instead of a hum, it was a grating sound, followed by a bang and a puff of smoke. The door opened and the

Digital Voodoo

compartment was empty.

"See, it really is a fake," Toma yelled. "Let's show him how we treat thieves at our spot on the river."

The Wish-maker twisted and pulled at the arm holding him fast. The villagers rushed the stage like a wave.

"No!" the Wish-maker yelled. With the fierceness of a trapped rat he kicked his captor in the knee, pulled free and fled before the mob. Toma was the last to follow. In the torch light his teeth gleamed like ice behind smiling lips.

Pedro helped Mama down. For a few minutes they stood listening to the shouts in the distance.

Pedro broke their silence, "Toma was right. I was foolish to drag you here. I didn't mean ..."

Mama cut him off, "Let's not speak of it. Tomorrow is another day. Come, let us go home, little man." She lowered her head allowing her hair to fall around it and held out her arm. Pedro slowly reached out for Mama.

"Wait Pedro," a quiet voice said. "Hello?"

"Who is it, Pedro?" Mama asked.

"I see no one."

The door to the magic box closed then opened, with a scraping sound.

"Please come here," the voice said.

"Mama, I think the magic box is calling me."

Mama let her arm slip from Pedro's grip but said nothing.

Pedro climbed aboard the wagon and tentatively stepped forward. Something black glinted inside the magic box. He bent closer peering into the dark opening.

"Take it," the voice said. "It will give your mother some sight."

Pedro moved the object around in his hands. A rectangular piece, skinny and about twice the width of his hand, seemed to be the main part. On either side were arms that flipped outward. Smooth and tapered they gently curved at the ends.

"It fits over the eyes and rests on the ears."

Pedro carried the gift gingerly to Mama. He examined the object and held it up to Mama's head. It fit like a blindfold over her eyes.

He stood in front of her, staring into the black eye cover. Mama was silent for a while.

"Oh, it tingles. Around the ears."

"Does it hurt?"

"No, but It's strange. I..."

Mama grabbed the device and froze. "Mama?"

She lifted her head. "Pedro, it's you?"

He wrapped Mama in his arms, lifting her from the ground. "You can see!" he screamed at the top of his lungs. "Mama can see!"

"How is it Mama? Isn't the world more beautiful than ever?"

"It is glorious and strange. You are a shadow made of many colors, with a strange gray light in your features. But I can tell it's you, and the village, and the trees, and the river."

She hugged her son even tighter.

"A moment, Mama," he said pulling away. He climbed back up to the magic box.

"Thank you for granting my wish."

"Yours was an unselfish request. The first I've had since being salvaged from the crash months ago. It was worthy of the sacrifice."

"Sacrifice?"

"Many of my internal components and sensors had to be cannibalized to make those. Your mother now sees heat, magnetic fields, and shapes, all combined into a composite that resembles optical sight."

"What?" Pedro shook his head at the babbling box.

"Simply put, I used parts of myself to make the thing that your mother is wearing."

"You sacrificed yourself for Mama's sight?"

"My power reserves were nearly depleted. I would not have been able to synthesize many more items. Not even the simple ones that the people of this planet need. In one or two of your days I would have ceased to function."

Pedro wondered what language the magic box spoke. Some of what it said was clear but most was nonsense. "Is there anything I can do for you?"

"No, leave me here and go about your business."

"Pedro!" Mama called. "The Wish-maker; we

must stop them."

With a gasp, Pedro leaped from the wagon. He took just a moment to look back at the magic box as it sat cold and silent, then he took off after his mother. She had already reached the edge of the river and was running along its bank.

Human Factors

This hall of the hospital, like all of them, glistened in antiseptic whiteness. The air the color of the wall, the flooring all exuded cool control. Allison Tourney walked briskly down through this environment mopping the sweat from her face with a kerchief. As she reached room four seventeen she handed the guard her ID card. Allison tapped her foot and looked around. The patient would leave and take his liability with him; the sooner the better.

The rising tide of heat continued to flood her body, starting from her chest and moving out to her limbs. Beads of sweat formed all over her body. She cursed under her breath. *I'm not old enough for menopause*, she thought.

"Allison Tourney, lead council, Prime Health." The guard read the holographic data from his hand-held security scanner, "You are cleared to enter." She entered the room shaking her head and muttering under her breath. The female tech, drawing blood from the patient's arm flinched. The patient turned his head to Allison, but he said nothing.

Allison watched the practiced hands of the tech as she removed the needle. Her hands, like her face, were smooth. Her jet black hair made wide looping curls down to her shoulders. She's so young. Clenching her fist, Allison looked to the patient. He filled the bed, with his feet just over the edge. The beds, in fact everything for the last forty years, had been designed for the average person.

Nothing about this man could be assumed to be normal. He had unremarkable features, dark hair, brown eyes, and looked to be in his twenties. She had been out of law school about ten years when he was born. With her career just blossoming and her husband's constant travel, it seemed unreasonable to have children. Year after year the excuses mounted until she became the childless old woman whose job was to eject this liability as quickly as possible, as if he were baggage. A man, who in another reality, could have been her son.

She clenched her fists tighter to force the thought from her mind. He was just another case and nothing else. With only a slight pause, she addressed the tech. "What are you doing?"

The tech was at the disposal chute breaking the needle from the vacutainer. The contaminated point was whisked away without breaking the seal. "Isn't it obvious?"

"You know that no sample can be taken from this man without written consent?"

The patient opened his mouth to speak but

was cut off by a quick gesture from Allison.

The tech faced Allison. "Dr. Zyger requested the sample."

A bluff, Allison was sure. She had been through too many cross examinations to miss the signs.

"Guard!" she called.

The guard entered the room, his hand on his side arm. Scanning the room he asked, "What's the problem here?"

"That remains to be seen. Just wait here a moment."

"What's going on here?" the patient asked, staring wide-eyed at the guard.

"Dr. Zyger will explain when he arrives." Her tone was final and he raised no objection.

Stepping to the wall intercom, she tapped the access button. The tired face of the duty nurse appeared, scowling at Allison.

"Ask Dr. Zyger to come to room 732, stat!" Without allowing the nurse to respond, she said, "Thank you," and switched off.

Allison faced the tech with the stern look she used to make witnesses squirm.

They waited in silence.

A few moments later Dr. Zyger burst into the room with lab coat fluttering in his wake, a shimmer of sweat on his face and balding head. Pushing the guard aside he dashed to the status board. It took only an instant for him to analyze the data. With a finger raised he turned on the tech. "There's no emergency!"

"I called you, Doctor," Allison interjected.

Zyger turned, malice in his eye. She had probably interrupted a time critical experiment that he would have to start over. He could have been mingling with philanthropists or a group of worshiping interns. One thing Allison was certain of, he was not doing vital work for any patient. "Stat is strictly for imminent terminal emergency, you know that," he said. "Misuse is a violation of hospital policy, which could lead to dismissal. Not even you are immune to that."

Allison shrugged nonchalantly. "Did you order a blood sample from this patient?"

"Why, I..." Zyger looked to the tech, her cheeks flushed and eyes desperate, then to Allison. "No," he muttered lowering his head.

Allison pressed toward the tech. "The sample," she said. Gently, the tubes were placed in her outstretched hand.

"That will be all, June," Zyger said, and the tech scurried from the room.

"You can go too," Zyger said to the guard, who shrugged and slipped out.

Allison went to the disposal chute. Without ceremony, she sent the sample through the one way flap to oblivion. It would soon be mixed with myriad other biological materials and chemicals, all to be incinerated.

"Excuse me, doctor," the patient said, waking Zyger from some dark reflection.

"Mr. Drexler, yes. Your condition, as you know, is not serious. You have a concussion, and some bruises and lacerations. You also have two broken fingers on your left hand. You're well enough to be discharged."

"As a matter of fact," Allison said, with a sidelong glance at Zyger, "your discharge papers are ready at the nurse's station."

"Mr. Drexler," Zyger paused in mid-sentence. "May I call you Otto?"

"If you like," came the quiet response.

Allison had always been irritated at the respect doctors got for simply being doctors. People wanted to trust them. As a lawyer she had to use every tool in her arsenal to overcome the basic mistrust of her profession.

Relaxing her posture she flashed her best motherly smile. "What do your friends call you?" she asked.

"Brother."

Although they waited for him to finish, nothing else came.

Dr. Zyger vigorously rubbed his forehead. He seemed perplexed. He pulled up a chair, sat on the edge and leaned in towards Otto. "Mr. Drexler, you are a very unusual man."

Otto shot a questioning glance at Allison; a show of confidence. Zyger seemed oblivious to the gesture. She had scored her first mark. Normally she tallied those points to gauge her effectiveness, but this time a song popped into her mind. A lullaby she used to sing to comfort her nephew. She flushed at the thought. *You're a professional*, she told herself.

Zyger continued, "The DNA of every new patient is micro scanned to find out which treatments are appropriate for them. Your DNA is unaltered, pristine in a sense."

"Is that unusual?"

"Well, yes. In all developed countries gene therapy starts well before birth. Within a month of fertilization the first normalization factors are introduced."

Otto's face paled. "People agree to that?"

"It's a benefit to the fetus. We've eliminated all forms of congenital birth defects. And as people age we're able to boost deficient immune systems. Most forms of cancer and heart disease are gone from the earth. Many diseases such as Alzheimer's have been eliminated from the population."

"When these adjustments are made to gene structures a flag is also set in the strand to identify the modification. Careful marking is important because remodifying a specific gene can cause unanticipated mutation to which the patient could have an adverse reaction."

Allison changed her stance. If Zyger got into his lecture mode it could go on for hours.

"I've read papers from doctors who have

worked with older patients who grew up without gene therapy. You appear to be much too young to be a part of that group. Where did you come from that didn't provide gene normalization?"

"I was born and raised at the Glory Ranch, a Faith Born colony in western Maryland!' The glow of his eyes reflected warm childhood memories.

"So, you know nothing of modern gene control methods!'

"We're not isolationists, Doctor. I've heard about such things. Many say that it's heresy to play with the makeup that God has given us."

"Otto, "Allison joined in. "What do you think?"

"God has given us intelligence, which we use to better our lives and the lives of others. The only problem I see is that it can bring people to relying on the arm of flesh."

"Arm of flesh?"

"You know, arm of flesh. Believing man is in control and disregarding the power of God."

Allison noticed Zyger shake his head. He was probably rolling his eyes as well. It was baby babble to him.

"Mr. Drexler, I've told you a little about modern gene therapy, but there is a barrier we haven't been able to cross."

Again Otto looked to Allison for help. Trying for a comforting smile, she looked into his soft brown eyes.

"You see, gene therapy adjusts human DNA towards a universal norm. Thus we call it gene normalization. This makes for a healthier, more well-adjusted population. By moving to this norm people develop the same basic size and build. They all have average intelligence and drive. Except for deformity, facial features are unaltered. Individuality is protected. And, of course environment, not genetics, is the major factor in the development of the personality. However this is a double edged sword. By eliminating Autism and Down's syndrome we have also removed the possibility of genius. We need a gene strand with a 'balancing factor: which was theorized about a decade ago, but has never been found in humans. Therefore we haven't been able to use our sequencers or other equipment to identify the gene that produces it."

Allison intruded on Zyger's lecture. "Otto, there are whole industries built around gene mining. From a DNA sample taken from one person they are able to extract, replicate, and store tens of thousands of gene factors, each to resolve some defect in human development. I must inform you of your rights at this point."

Zyger leaned back in his chair with a heavy sigh.

Allison brushed it off and began her own lecture. "The gene rights act of 2028 grants all individuals exclusive rights to their DNA. No one can appropriate, use, patent, or market any genes or gene factors derived from an individual without the permission of that individual. The individual is also entitled to compensation for transferring this right to any person or entity. Dr. Zyger is about to inform you that your DNA is in high demand and will want you to grant our hospital research rights to your DNA."

Zyger jumped to his feet. "Why don't you just tell him to go away. Whose side are you on anyway?"

"My job is to protect the hospital and parent corporation from liability. Direct and concise disclosure is the only way of gaining informed consent that will hold up in court. I have been doing this job for more than thirty years, doctor. I know what will stand up and what won't."

Zyger started pacing around the room rubbing his forehead. "As Ms. Tourney has blurted out, we would like rights to research your DNA. You'd be compensated handsomely."

"Why, what's so special about my DNA?"

Zyger walked to Otto's side. "You have the balancing factor. Within your DNA we can advance mankind beyond the species' current limitations. Developing whole populations with intelligence, grace, strength, or any other feature at a level never dreamed of before. Think of it. The man of the future will be as distant from us as we are from the apes. What took nature millennia to do, we could complete in four generations. Wouldn't you want to be part of that? You'd become the father of the next evolution of mankind."

Otto's face contorted with thought. Allison

couldn't tell what his reaction was, but definitely not the enthusiasm of Zyger.

"It's quite a bit to think about, isn't it?" Allison asked.

Otto looked up at Allison, his eyes intense. "Isn't what God made good enough? We were created in His image; what could be better?"

Allison gently rested on the edge of the bed. "Otto, I'm a lawyer representing the interests of the hospital. Within that context I will help you as much as possible." She swallowed hard. "But the questions you're asking are beyond the scope of my specialties. You have been given the facts. The decision is yours." She gently patted his hand. The warmth of it penetrated her palm. She had often held her nephew's hand, when they played or when she had read to him. His hand just fit in hers. That had been before her sister moved. For three years Allison had missed the touch of her substitute son.

She snapped to, as if from a dream, and pulled back.

They all sat in silence for a few moments. Otto switched his gaze to the doctor.

"It's the chance of a lifetime, my boy," Zyger said with a broad smile.

Another moment passed before Otto spoke. "Could I have a few minutes alone please?"

"Certainly," Allison said, rising from the bed. She met his eyes as they left.

Outside they found a quiet corner to talk in.

"He's going to agree," Zyger stated.

"By the look of him, he's nowhere near a decision."

"It's the opportunity of a lifetime, how could he turn it down?"

"Didn't you see it in his eyes? He'll be struggling with it for days."

"The balancing factor cannot develop in a populace where genes are controlled with the precision inherent in modern medical treatment. We may never find another one like him. He has to agree."

"We've developed a credible consent claim. If he agrees, we should have no problems. But we can't force him. It would leave us open to liability beyond what Prime Health can bear. It's in his hands, not yours."

Zyger's mood seemed to darken as she spoke. She had seen him in many temperamental moods but never so withdrawn.

They went to get coffee and spent the next few minutes silently nurturing their own thoughts.

Finally Zyger announced it was time to check in on the patient.

Entering the room they found Otto kneeling beside the bed, head bowed.

"What in the world?" Zyger mumbled. He stepped forward reaching for the crouched figure. "Young man ..."

Allison yanked on his arm. He turned to see

her holding a finger to her lips. He stood up quizzically gesturing.

"He's praying," she whispered.

Zyger's eyebrows shot up, then contracted with a frown. He gestured with his hands, obviously asking, "What now?"

"Haven't you ever been to church?" she asked.

He looked befuddled, rubbing his forehead lightly. She took him by the arm, drawing him towards the door. They were stopped by Otto's voice.

"Amen," the voice said, single and clear. He sat up on the bed and she recognized his expression. She had trained herself to see it in jurors, from their expressions, their body language, to know when they were convinced on a particular point. Otto had decided.

Zyger spoke up, "Well, Mr. Drexler, with a chance to reflect upon it, you've decided to help I trust?"

"Dr. Zyger, I'm sorry to disappoint you, but I can't."

"But of course you can. All we need is a small sample to run tests on and it won't hurt. We're not cloning you or anything like it. This is a tightly supervised industry. There can be no misuse of your genetic materials. You're completely covered from litigation."

"How can you say there will be no legal actions? A couple of years back our colony was sued by a group of tourists. They claimed that the column of smoke rising from a fire we had built spoiled their view of the 'pristine' landscape. If litigation can be formed around something as trivial as that, how can you stop something as far-reaching as this?"

Zyger looked to Allison with a wry smile.

Yes, it was her job, but she hated the way people expected her to jump through hoops like a trained animal when it suited them. "Otto, as part of the gene mining laws you are immune to any litigation, criminal or civil, as a result of any outcome of the application of any developments derived from your DNA. The entity, corporate or private, that acquires the rights to your genetic material assumes all liability for its use, intentional or inadvertent."

Otto seemed to think about it for a moment. Immunity from litigation was a panacea everyone dreamed of. Average Americans would be in court at least ten times during their lives, and usually a postmortem case.

Zyger's smile broadened. Just a hint of respect showed through. More than half of all procedures performed by doctors became the basis of a lawsuit or two. Only twenty percent of the cases Allison defended made it past the plausibility hearing, a record envied by many hospital legal departments.

Zyger showed every confidence that with her help this would be the hook to catch Otto.

After a moment Otto turned to Zyger. "I understand that you consider this a good and important thing. You're committed to the world of science: see, hear, feel, measure, and record. I'm committed to a different world, where faith and inspiration are our guiding tenets. I've been praying and the Lord has revealed to me that this is wrong."

Zyger's eyes became severe, although his tone was steady. "What do you mean, 'wrong: Was it wrong for man to develop the steam engine, or the airplane, or vaccines, or organ transplants? The advancement of science brings health and prosperity to all mankind."

"Doctor, I appreciate all that man has been able to discover and put to use. The ability to gain knowledge and to use it creatively are gifts from God. They can be used in positive and good ways or in ways that aren't. The Lord is the one who can tell us. Listen to Him, Doctor Zyger. He will let you know."

Zyger's voice rose a notch. "This is your chance to be written into the history books!"

Otto quietly responded, "The book of life is the only one that counts."

"Otto, you're in real danger. The tech that was in here earlier and others already know of your DNA. It won't be long before someone comes for you. They'll take the DNA and possibly leave you dead. Your cult can't save you. We have the proper connections, corporate and government. You'll be safe with us. Please, I don't want to see you get hurt."

"Doctor, whether I live or die is up to God. I can only choose how I live my life. I can't help you and serve God too."

"You're part of the family of man and have a responsibility to share your gifts with the rest of your race. Can't you see that this is more important than you or me? It's obvious that this religion thing is significant to you but sacrifices must be made for the future of mankind?"

Allison broke in, "Dr. Zyger! That will be enough. Any further effort on your part would be construed as undue pressure and would undermine our consent claims. You may have already gone too far."

Zyger buried his shaking head in his hands. After a moment he stood up, with a sigh, and quietly lumbered from the room.

Releasing the breath she had been holding, she turned to Otto. "You're ready for discharge now." She pressed the button that activated the opaque screen around his bed.

He began changing behind the curtain. "You're a good person. Thank you for everything."

Many responses ran through Allison's mind, *just doing my job or I did what the law required.* She said, "You're welcome. Don't be concerned about Zyger. He's not a bad man, just very wrapped up in his research. You shouldn't worry about his threat either. I'll see that your records are destroyed. I have the authority to do that."

"He was rather intense, but the Lord loves him like the rest of his children."

"You have an unusual outlook on life."

"How is that?"

"Well, most people would jump at the money. It's a difficult world and cash makes it much easier."

"Ms. Tourney, when you have peace in your heart the world is not difficult."

She seemed to burn with his words; another hot flash. I'll wait for you outside," she said, rising and heading for the door.

Some cold water might help so she looked down the hall for the water bubbler. As she looked for it she saw Dr. Zyger through the nurses' library window. He was on the phone. Allison knew he was challenging her decision with her supervisor or the chairman of the board. She brushed concerns of Zyger away and headed for the bubbler.

It was only a few minutes later when Otto emerged from the room. He was dressed very simply, his look understated. Maybe a suit or ensemble would make him a striking figure, but he appeared as just a man. Allison shook her head and brought out a smile to greet him.

They walked down the corridor exchanging pleasantries. Allison saw Zyger from the corner of her eye. He was off the phone. He stepped out and joined them but didn't look at Otto.

"Young man, could I not prevail upon you to change your mind?"

Otto shrugged and smiled. Allison noted how the gesture brought out small dimples on his cheeks.

At the exit Allison wanted to touch Otto's arm, to stop him and say something profound. Maybe to kiss him and wish him luck. She watched as he went through the double doors and mumbled, "Take care of yourself." The child she never had was walking out of her life.

Doctor Zyger stood beside her in silence.

As she stood in a numb void, Otto was thrown to the ground by three men. People began running in all directions, scurrying from the scene. A high pitched scream cut the air. Only after did Allison realize it was her own. She watched as Otto beat back his attackers. He was strong and nimble. Allison began to hope he would fend them off.

The security guard came down to the end of the corridor with a growing mass of people. The hospital litigation insurance only covered him within the walls of the hospital. There were no deep pockets to protect him outside. He could lose his job, besides being sued for all that he had. They had all been programmed by litigation. Anyone who got involved in someone else's problem only brought disaster on themselves.

Allison watched with the rest of the crowd, frozen by the primal display of violence.

A punch landed on Otto's jaw and sent him reeling backward. The dull thud of fist against face penetrated the door and released Allison from her shock. She pulled open the door and started to run out.

She felt resistance on her arm. Looking back, she saw Zyger attempting to restrain her. With all her might she pressed on pulling Zyger off balance. Allison ran out onto the sidewalk with Zyger tumbling out behind her.

She came to the closest attacker. As he attempted to lift himself from the ground she kicked him in the face causing him to fall back down.

As she turned to find Otto, her hopes were dashed in a single instant. One of the attackers had a gun. It seemed in slow motion. The gun came up as she ran towards the man. She only needed a second or two to cover the distance. The gun came up and pointed directly at Otto. She leaped at the assassin but just before her body made contact a shot rang out.

She and the beast fell together in a crumpled heap. Allison tried to strike him but he pushed her off.

At that moment a siren split the air. The Police were near. She allowed herself a slight glimmer of hope. Moving her head around to find Otto she saw Zyger standing in front of him, a red stain growing across the front of his lab coat.

# # #

Allison pulled back the curtains in Doctor Zyger's hospital room. He raised a hand to shield his eyes from the afternoon sun.

"You have a visitor," she said without any inflection of voice.

He only grunted.

Crossing the room, she exited for a moment and came back in with Otto.

Zyger folded his arms across his chest, gently.

Otto walked up to the bed and held out his hand. "I wanted to thank you for saving my life."

Zyger paused for an instant but took the hand. "Thankful enough to give me a sample of your blood?" Zyger cocked his head to one side.

"Now," Otto responded, "we've gone over this before. I can't support your research, but I've helped as much as I can."

Zyger rubbed his forehead. "What does that mean?"

Otto and Allison shared a glance and Otto said, "Well, I must be going." With that he left the room and their lives.

Allison stood at the foot of Zyger's bed, staring at the man.

"What?"

"You should be in a prison hospital."

Zyger looked away.

"The only reason you are not is because Otto refused to press charges. He appreciates that you saved his life and is willing to overlook the fact that you called those thugs down on him. He calls it forgiveness."

Allison stared at the man for a few more

seconds and strode towards the door. She was stopped just before the door by Zyger's voice.

"Wait," he called. "What did he mean that he's helped as much as he could?"

Biting her lip Allison weighed telling him the truth. As she considered the options she ultimately decided that he would probably find out sooner or later.

Turning to Zyger she took a deep breath. "You and Otto have the same blood type."

"So?" Zyger responded.

"So, you lost a lot of blood and Otto decided to donate to assist in your recovery."

Zyger seemed confused for a moment and then his eyes opened wider and he smiled.

"Don't you dare smile!" Allison ordered, wiping his expression clear. "You almost got the boy killed."

Allison turned from Zyger's blank stare and marched from the room. Outside she took out a kerchief and stared at it blankly for a moment before starting to mop up the sweat on her face.

ODDS ON REVENGE

Kamen strutted into the bedroom, his smile glistening in the darkness. Protective shielding kept him safe from snipers and diffusion glass from spies. There was no reason to keep it dark, but the dark was his friend. Looking out on the hue and glitter of the city he could imagine himself sultan, the game master of the world. Yes, even the masters would worship him as the ruler of chance.

His routine was to open the door, stride seven steps in, and jump, lofting himself into the feathered softness of the bed. The comforter and bedding would fly up, burying him as it gently settled back. He savored it like a cat.

He was on step six when the door closed. The quiet rustle of clothing came from behind him.

"Who's in here?" Kamen demanded as he turned.

The figure remained consumed in the shadows.

"Lights!" Kamen called. Nothing happened.

"I've learned some stuff since we last met," came a man's voice.

137

"Who are you? What are you doing in my place?"

The man moved from the shadow enough for Kamen to make out the silhouette. The intruder had a handgun. "Let's just say, I'm an unhappy mark come to repay ya."

Kamen folded his arms over his chest and gazed harder at the shadow. "Look, bum, you take your chances at the games, just like everyone else. Take your losses like a man. You know, I've had a good day, and I'm in a generous mood. So, I'm willing to cut you a break. I'll turn my back and go to bed. If you're out of my suite before I get there, I'll forget you were ever here."

"No dice."

"You know there are worse things than death. I can make sure you experience each and every one of them over the next decade or so. Why don't you just run along, before I get ugly?"

"Been there, done that. Now it's your turn."

Kamen took a few steps back and sat on the foot of his bed. Bums and losers were irritating, never seeming to know what was best for them.

"Okay, let's say that you actually have the guts to kill me. The security in this place will be down on you in ten seconds. Barely time to get to the door. You'd never get out alive."

"What makes ya think I intend to survive?"

The shadow tossed an object into the light. About the size of a grapefruit it rolled to within a meter of Kamen. He knew little about ordnance, but recognized it as a remote activated bomb, big enough to incinerate everything in the room.

Kamen's fingers sunk like daggers into the mattress. "Okay, buddy, let's think about this. There's nothing to gain by killing both of us. You'd have no chance to gloat, to relish in your accomplishment."

"Lights!" called the figure, and the lights sprang to life.

"You control my systems?" If he controlled the lights, he may have the defensive systems too, projectiles, gas, stunners. Kamen's dinner turned in his stomach.

"Now, how's about you and me talk."

The man wore baggy clothes, worn with patches on patches, and none of it was clean. The creature smiled. The few teeth he had were crooked and gray, a beard scragged about his face.

Kamen shook his head. "Who are you?"

"Let me refresh your memory." The man pulled up his sleeve revealing a black and red brand.

"I've never owned a slave, what's that supposed to mean to me?"

"How many do ya sell into slavery?"

"Well," Kamen coughed. "Common practice in a high stakes game. The masters are the ones that deal in slaves. I only play games. Besides, you had to agree to the stakes before the game. Full disclosure and what not."

"How many Kamen? You can't remember me

because I'm just one of hundreds, or thousands?" His voice rose as he spoke. "Look at me!"

Kamen stared into the man's face. Wrinkled, with some scars, it barely appeared human. "Sorry," he said, shaking his head.

"Bomb, activate!"

"No!" Kamen jumped from his bed and lunged towards the door.

The man struck him on the shoulder with the side of the gun. Pinpricks sprinkled down the right half of Kamen's body and he fell with a thud. He lay on the floor, his right arm and leg twitching uncontrollably.

The man leaned over him. Gently he said, "Neat, huh? Nobody's going to wrestle this away from me in a fight. One of them genetic keys."

Kamen only groaned.

"Ya got a nicer place here. I remember the old dump. Yup, got it all locked up in here." The man tapped the side of his head with the gun. "Kamen's game room was hardly better than the rest of the dives, but ya played high stakes. When did ya move up town?"

Kamen's body settled down, but he didn't respond.

"It's great what a hacker can do. Even transfer savings into junk bonds, or commodities, or one of them start-up companies that die in their first year." The man smiled.

"What do you want?" Kamen groaned.

"That's more like it. See, we can work things out. All we've got to do is talk like gentlemen." He stood and forced his toe under Kamen's chest. With a pointed thrust he rolled Kamen over onto his back.

"I've gone over it, in my mind, for the past eighteen years. The only way for you to win that game was to cheat. So what I want is a game, a fair game."

"I never cheat."

"Very well, let's play." The intruder pulled out a deck of Caso cards.

"Here? Now?"

"That's right. You, me, and a deck. We play one hand. Ya win; I take my bomb and go away. I win and I do to ya what ya did to me."

Kamen burned as a chill swept over his body.

"Ya were happy to take me on before."

Kamen stared at the man, chin firm. In high stakes a gambler wagered his freedom against a fortune to last the rest of his life. Kamen had always been the house, risking monetary loss.

"The masters, they worship randomness, chaos, whatever. Games of chance are religious ceremonies to them, and a rigged game is sacrilege."

Kamen shrugged.

"You're a big man with the masters. The player who can't lose. Heck, you're the closest thing they got to a prophet. What do ya think they'll do to ya when they find out you're a fraud?"

"The masters know that I run a clean game. Accusations from a loser will be discarded without consideration."

"Got it all figured, Kamen? What the heck, what's to lose? And if ya win, I'll go with all my embarrassing questions."

"How do I know that you'll keep your end, once I've won?"

The man wrapped his fingers into Kamen's collar and twisted, forcing his fist into Kamen's throat. "I'm not the guy who cheats kids out of their lives. Ya don't get it. I'm going to beat ya fair and square. Just to show ya that in a fair game, you'd lose."

Kamen was wheezing, gasping for breath as the man drug him from the floor and led him into the living room. The man sat him down at the gaming table. Then took the opposite chair. He set the gun by his right hand and the bomb to his left, and began shuffling the cards.

"Now, ya cut, I deal."

"Wait a moment. You shuffled. Even if I cut you can deal yourself anything you want."

The man's smile became icy. "House rules, remember."

Kamen swallowed. Forcing all doubt back, he reminded himself that the bum couldn't possibly win.

The man passed the deck to Kamen, who tapped the top to pass. It was rigged, cutting made no difference.

"Ya sure ya want to pass?"

"Deal the cards."

The cards flew back and forth, building two piles. He was good; Kamen couldn't see him pulling from the bottom of the deck. Kamen had seen the best, but this bum was smooth.

Kamen's hand was average. A pair of Otans would let him take the early lead, unless the bum had dealt himself a Ritdan.

Kamen sat back and steadied his head. Looking over his hand he focused on the bum's cards. The nano-machines that made up his ocular implant whirred about in his retina. Instantly he was locked in on the back of the cards. Auto ranging would handle the focus from then on. He relaxed as the micro sensors brought back images of the inside of the cards. In a moment he would be locked onto the printing on the other side of the cards. His pleasure was only manifest by a slight rise of his pulse.

The final image entered his brain as a cobweb of random figures. The lines and figures seemed to swirl in a way that made him dizzy. They flowed around a central point where a single word was written: loser.

Kamen stiffened and sucked in a quick breath. Immediately he knew it was a mistake. Come on idiot, he chided himself. Perfect demeanor was one of his trademarks. He looked up to see the bum's smile broaden.

Kamen touched his chest, scrunched his face a little and said, "gas."

The bum continued to smile. "Your play," he

said.

Kamen focused on his hand. He'd have to win this the old fashioned way. The bum probably expected him to lead with the Otan. The Otans could be held in reserve and sprung when least expected. It's anticipating the opponent that leads to victory. The rest of the cards were unremarkable. Kamen threw out an Inti, a mid level card, forcing the bum to play higher to take it.

Another Inti came flashing out of the bum's hand. Kamen sat back. The bum's face was ice, too good to give anything away.

"Okay," Kamen said reviewing his cards. He could throw a lower card and give up the trick or play higher to draw out a larger card. The bum was good at dealing and holding his face, but only amateurs match cards early in the game. With a stacked deck he could be leading to a single trick game, constantly matching, then topping at the end.

That suited Kamen well; he could build up and use the pair of Otans to double trump. With a stacked deck he was sure to lose anyway. Why not go out in a blaze of glory. Kamen threw a Jentax, two points up.

Another Jentax, just like he figured. The bum was predictable; it would be easy to finish him off.

Kamen added a Lim, starting to move into powerful cards.

Instead of another Lim the bum threw a Mokko, the trick was his. Obviously he had miscounted cards or something. Mokkos were closing cards, saved to the end.

The bum sorted through the trick.

"Remember, you can't put the Mokko back in your hand," Kamen said.

The bum's gray face stared back at him, behind glistening eyeballs. "I'm here to win, not to cheat." He threw the Mokko across the floor. It landed leaning against the base of the bar. "Your play," he said.

Kamen hadn't lost any valuable cards in the exchange. He shrugged it off. He would pull out the bum's strategy with conservative play. He tossed an Aublek, lowest of the low.

The bum sucked it up with a Lim, and quickly added it to his hand.

"Too bad you haven't got as much strategy as you have guts."

The bum smiled, "It's my game."

The bum didn't seem to have a strategy. He sacrificed good solid middleweight cards to pick up the lowest level. The bum's hand grew as Kamen's shrunk. The bum obviously didn't realize the advantage of being the one going down. Kamen smiled inwardly keeping his face stone.

Three cards left and his lead. Kamen shuffled them around in his hand and his mind. Ether and two Otans, he shouldn't split the pair, but if he led with the Ether he may be forced to throw one of the Otans. If he did that and the bum captured it, he'd lose for sure.

Kamen tossed out the Ether.

Instantly the bum countered with another Ether, the dolt! No one in his right mind would counter facing just three cards. The bum just threw the game. Kamen's heart took a sudden leap. He forced his breathing down. As soon as he played the Otan the bum would try to take the trick. The stupid fool thinks he's won the game. Kamen couldn't wait to see the reaction when he trumped with the pair of Otans.

A long droning sigh came from Kamen as he tried to sound dejected. The Otan landed gently on the Ethers.

A snorting laugh arose from the bum as he tossed another Ether on the Otan. "Trump!" he called.

Kamen allowed himself a grin. The drama played out; the last card was his winner. He threw it down, staring at his opponent's face. "Trump, this!"

The bum's face went slack. He looked up to Kamen, solid and severe. "Okay" he said and threw another Ether on the pile.

Blood drew from Kamen's face as the card fell. "A triple, a triple! You lousy, cheating bum." Slam, Kamen's chair hit the floor as he bolted up. "All right, where are you keeping them?"

"What?" the bum played ignorant.

"You're not fooling me. This match is invalid, I will not be bound by its outcome." Kamen slammed his fist on the table.

"I'm no cheater. Ya don't like to lose, tell ya what. We play again, double or nothing."

"Why would I want to play with cheating scum like you?"

"Ya deal this time."

Kamen paused in mid rant. "What about house rules?"

"House just made new rules." The bum smiled his ragged smile.

"What do you have in mind?"

"Ya win, I leave. I win, I get all ya stuff." He waved his hand around. "Everything."

"If I deal, I get to use my own deck?"

"I'm your guest. Do as you please."

Kamen raced to the bar and pulled a deck from behind it. He usually kept it there for party tricks. A quick scan revealed that they were unaltered; he'd be able to read through them. "All right then, let's see if you can do it twice."

Kamen played to the bum's hand, drawing out the mid level cards and eating up everything else. He thought about how he would come down on that bum. Simple execution would be too good. No, he'd have him sent back to the slave pits, with an additional infirmity, unable to defend himself.

The game went quickly. Kamen was down to his last card, a Zetto, the only one in the deck. Considering it was his lead, there was nothing the bum could do. He tossed it down. "Nice game. Now, why don't you get out of my place."

The bum slowly took the gun and placed it in his jacket pocket. Grabbing the bomb he lifted it in his left hand. It clicked and whined as he pressed a button.

"Wait, look you made the rules. You said that you'd keep your end of the bet. I don't want any trouble."

The bum put the bomb on the table and looked up at Kamen. "Ya have a strange way of trying to avoid it."

The lights on the bomb faded. "No hard feelings though," Kamen sputtered. "Please take a bottle of something with you on your way out." He'd have the bum followed. A few blocks away he'd be stunned and tossed into a trunk, packaged for a trip to agony.

The bum gently pulled at the sides of the bomb, and it fell in half. An elliptical black device was inside.

"I'm certain that you can find better places to play with your toys."

The bum stroked it. "No, this is the best place for this toy. Don't know its real name. Let's just call it a master-cam."

Ice ran through Kamen's veins. "A what?"

"It's a device the masters use to check for cheating. It tracks the relative position of every card within three meters."

Kamen turned up the corner of his mouth in

a smile of malice. "I played a perfectly fair game. Not one chard was taken from my sleeve, or palmed, or stacked, or dealt from the bottom. Now, as I was saying: take your toy and..."

"This one has a special modification," the bum interrupted. "It has an electro-magnetic signature tracker."

Kamen's fists clenched.

"As you know, a dampening field around the table blocks normal surveillance equipment, so peeking over someone's shoulder has been eliminated. Other counter measures keep resonance based and electronic marking from being effective."

Kamen walked to the bar. Directly behind the bum he wrapped his hand around a pewter decanter of tonic. The metal leached any warmth left in his fingers.

The stupid bum kept on babbling, unaware or not caring that Kamen was about to crush his skull in. He would claim it was self-defense. The bum went wild after he lost. The device, which Kamen never knew was anything but a bomb, just happened to be crushed in the struggle. Kamen's smile returned.

"But, you can't block visible light or the players can't see to play the game. So, I figured that you had to be using some kind of advanced optical analyzer."

The statement froze Kamen at the top of his swing. Could he really have figured it out? The only other people who knew, including the inventor, were dead.

Kamen quickly ran through the odds. His best chance was to kill the intruder and go with his story.

The metal club arched down upon its victim. It landed with a delightful thud. Blood oozed from the wound as the body slumped over the table. Kamen struck again and again, making sure to finish the job. He would need to have the place cleaned, he thought as he wiped the blood on his robe. Turning the decanter over, he opened it and poured himself a drink.

The door slid open with a hushed sound. The tall angular body of a master entered, surrounded by three men. Kamen dropped his drink. The glass shattered on the floor.

The door was the only way out. The protective windows were sealed shut. Under the bed, in the closet, there was no place to hide.

"You should have let him finish," came the synthetic voice of the master.

"He attacked me..." Kamen stuttered. "It was self-defense."

He thought of the shattered glass on the floor. "I only needed the drink to steady my nerves before calling for security."

"Your victim was about to say that the device transmitted its data to us in the next room. The whole event was viewed by us, and recorded. We even managed to identify your ocular implant."

Kamen gripped the nearest chair to steady

himself. The men closed in on him. He had trained himself to look defeated, vulnerable. It built confidence in his opponents.

The closest man reached out to take his arm. Kamen swung around the chair, hitting the man in the side and lunged through the opening.

Time to retire. He ran for the door. Once on the streets he'd disappear. There was enough hidden cash to sustain him in a low profile.

The master stood in the doorway. Kamen allowed himself a grin. Their technology allowed them to conquer the galaxy, but one on one they were weaklings.

Kamen bowled into the ribbon body of the master. They fell through the doorway in a heap. It may have been a mistake, Kamen realized. In a second the thugs were on him. He thrashed and kicked at the body and arms of the master. In an instant he rolled free.

As he jumped to his feet, the master shoved something in his face with a mist spraying from it. It was sweet almost sticky and caused him to cough. He leaped away and headed down the hall. He still had a good chance to get away. The emergency chute was a meter away when he fell to the ground. His body twitched for a few seconds before it lay still.

His arms and legs numbly sat on the floor. He heard footsteps closing on him, but his body was limp. "Move, move!" he yelled. But his limbs lay still.

The eel-like face of the master came into view

as he was rolled over.

"Don't worry. The effects are not permanent. You will soon be fully able to work in your slave hold."

"Wait, I've got money. I'll make you rich, all of you, just let me go."

The master clicked-out something in its own language and spit upon Kamen.

"It was a setup all along. But, why didn't you stop it before I killed your stooge."

"It was his wish. As a valuable slave, he would not have been allowed to die. Utterly wasteful."

Kamen's face went white and he began mumbling incoherently.

"That's right, Kamen, humans are simple to repair. A little maintenance and you'll go on forever too."

"But, what about my money, homes, belongings? The bum can't.." Kamen trailed off.

"He played the first game fair, no cheating, so legally it all belongs to him."

"He's dead."

"Yes, but as his estate it goes to his sister. His only living relative."

"The sap," Kamen said.

The master kicked Kamen in the ribs. "He is a hero. He played pure chance and skill, and won his death. Do not speak of him again. Your vile tongue is not worthy of his name."

With that, the master reared to his full height

and Kamen was dragged off to eternity.

Flash Fiction:

These stories are less than one thousand words each. Some are only a few hundred words long. These are like the one minute mysteries of fiction. And, yes, not all of these are science fiction or fantasy.

Blades

The Sun was setting on the white cloven hills. Long shadows stretched across the frozen lake. The pink glare of sunset flashed on their blades as the mob cut and slashed among their adversaries. The frost, which bit the air, marked hair white and their faces red. These stark contrasts made them almost seem to belong in this frozen wilderness. Savage, wild, and unforgiving.

As the struggle raged on shouts and screams filled the air, broke the mood of silent winter. Steam rose off their bodies with the efforts to push past the defenders. Jason standing half a head taller than the others took a second to survey the scene. Soon the sun would be down and distinguishing friend from foe would be a challenge. They needed to end this now.

Then he saw it, an opening. He raced forward, slamming the only one in his way to the ground and called to his fellows. A cheer rang out.

He had broken through the ranks of defenders. Now only one man lay between him and his goal. He wound up and let loose with the most vicious stroke of his life.

The puck flew right between the goalie's pads. A score, they won 5 to 4. Just in time too. Jason's mother was calling him in for dinner.

The Fall

"I am a fake!" Connie yelled as she slipped backwards off the windowsill. She sensed the hundreds of feet of open space beneath her. It would only take a few seconds to hit bottom, but time seemed to have slowed.

"It's not real," she told herself. Even the hair wasn't real as the wind rustled it flowing in golden rivulets about her face. The clouds and sky watched calmly as she fell. She marveled at the perception of distance. The building rushed by like a rocket, while the azure sky stood peaceful, as always.

Connie's mother called it a cult. Something evil she shouldn't go near. But Connie embraced it. She wasn't sure when it had become her goal, but she managed it with the help of her new friends.

It wouldn't be long now. Her friends had told her what to expect on impact, a dizzying array of blue, yellow, and white. Then it would be over. Their late night planning sessions would be consummated in this one brief instant.

And then in an instant, it was over. She felt the impact and tried to scream, but nothing came out.

"Cut!" the director called. Connie pulled herself out of the landing mat. "That was a beautiful, first fall honey," he said with a wink. Turning to the crew he hollered, "Okay, get Miss Goldilocks out here for the close-up."

Expectations

She leaned over her pot. It bubbled and churned just like the one on the television. She had struggled before with this recipe but never seemed to get it right. He would be there soon and she wasn't ready.

The Host seemed to go through the dicing and measuring, mixing and stirring with a light air. She, on the other hand, struggled. With her hair frizzed out by the steam she looked wild and frazzled.

Wiping the sweat from her face she pressed the play button again. The DVD player had been such a help. She silently thanked the creators of the unique device. Technology amazed her as she never seemed to grasp how it could possibly work.

The work was mostly done with a few more pinches and some stirring. Pinches were always used, but she struggled to approximate the amount used by the host. She took up a bit of the ground herb and rubbed it between her fingers, as the host did. But, she let it fall back into the container. Squinting at the screen she ran back the show to see what the pinch looked like as it fell and compared it to her efforts.

Foot steps, she heard foot steps out in her yard. It was him. She started and dropped the container. The steps were on the porch now. Bending down she took a pinch from the floor and hastily threw it into the pot.

Without knocking the man entered. He was tall, thin, and seemed middle age, very nondescript.

Without a word he walked over to the pot and sniffed. Removing a small notebook from his pocket he jotted down a note. Next he took the spoon and stirred it a few times. He even scooped up some of the liquid and let it fall back into the pot.

Making another note he turned to face the woman. "This is your third and final chance to pass the potion's test. If you fail this time you will not be worthy to become a witch."

"I've done everything correctly," she said with a curtsy.

He sniffed. "This is the frog potion, isn't it?"

"Yes," she smiled. "Anyone who drinks even a little of it will be turned into a frog."

"Very well," he jotted another note. "Drink some."

"Drink some?"

"Yes, you heard me. Or do you think I'm going to test it for you?"

"No, no," she sputtered.

With a trembling hand she took up the spoon with a small amount of potion in it, closed her eyes and swallowed.

In the blink of an eye she was transformed into a frog, green and damp, looking up into the eyes of the man.

He made a final note in his book, pocketed it, turned and headed for the door.

She croaked at him.

He turned. "Witches don't do what they are told, you silly woman. You failed the test." He paused. "Well, technically, if you manage to find some way to transform yourself back, you can have one more try."

With that the man left.

The woman trapped in a frog's body croaked.

Contrail

The pure blue sky was only marred by one streak of gold, a contrail tainted by the setting sun. As he looked upon it, his fists unconsciously tightened. Most people would think it pretty, a ribbon across the sky. He, however, scowled at it, blocking out the background noise, and scowled with all the force he could muster.

He had been in planes many times, some large, some small, and many in-between. He had even been in a helicopter more than once. It wasn't his job to fly, but his work required constant travel. If only he had gotten frequent flier miles, he'd have enough to retire on. Maybe one day, he thought, but shook his head. That day would never come. Retirement was a fantasy he wouldn't live to see. The noise over his shoulder grew louder.

Looking down he took stock of himself; nothing but the clothes he wore and a single side arm. The noise grew to the point that he could make out individual voices, yelling in a language he didn't understand. He un-balled his fists and examined his hands. They were his living, his bread and butter, but they could do nothing for him now.

He smiled and said, "My bread and butter," but he couldn't hear his own voice over the din. It seemed such a comforting and sweet phrase, one that didn't fit his situation at all.

Looking up to the contrail, he pulled himself to attention and saluted the last flight out of Saigon.

The Verdict

George looked around the court room. The jury had just taken their seats and none would make eye contact with him. It didn't look good. He had expected it but hoped for better.

He was a scientist. He developed new technology to help humanity. He never intended for anyone to he hurt. But now they feared him and it.

It was wrong, he knew, for them to stifle his creative energy. What right did any of them have to restrict his activity? He worked for their benefit, so they were only hurting themselves. No matter what the verdict...

He took a deep breath and willed his heart to beat more slowly. It was that sort of thinking that got him into this trouble.

They were all called to rise as the judge entered the court room. He didn't make eye contact either.

George looked at his feet for a minute and wondered if he had doomed not only himself but his colleagues. What would happen to the research, the new technology they developed over the last year? It promised so much. Surely, the judge would recognize this.

His attorney rose with him as the jury

foreman prepared to read the verdict. George concentrated on the piece of paper that held his future written on it. His knees shook and he felt beads of sweat form on his brow.

"In the case of Humanity versus Technology we the jury find Technology guilty."

The room erupted in applause and cheers. George fell into his seat. Just because the first prototype of his steam-engine exploded didn't mean that he couldn't resolve the pressure issue. It would revolutionize transportation and manufacturing and who knew what else.

He realized that the judge was speaking.

"Development of any technology beyond what we have now is forbidden. Anyone found to be delving into these evil arts will be sentenced to 20 years hard labor, just like the defendant here."

The gavel came down with a crack.

The Curse of Metal

He had once been perfect. His metal body the height of design and excellence, suited to his tasks. That had been long ago.

The family he was made for - the Willywigs - had passed him down from generation to generation, from the original (Old John) right through to his great-great grandson Tibby. He had no feelings, as he knew the humans did. He saw their care and concern for one another, even for him. Although he could not share in their love he accepted his position and felt a certain comfort in it. He didn't know how it would feel or if it would matter to him, if he were sold. But he thought it would be better to stay with the Willywigs as they had depended on him for years.

Would it be useful if he could feel? He wondered if it would allow him to help the family more. If he cared, would the output of his work increase, would he be able to listen and give good advice to the children? Would it help him to understand their needs? Would they be missing him?

At that point in his existence it mattered little. It had been a few days since he had seen his owners. He had aged, not in human terms but in terms of metal. It was true that he remained shiny on the outside, but his joints had taken to the curse of metal, rust. He needed frequent lubrication to remain limber, to do his job.

It was unfortunate that he hadn't lubricated himself more fully. He stood frozen in his metal body unable to help the Willywigs, nor even to care about the fact that he was stuck. He would probably remain where he was until his whole form succumbed to the disease.

As he stood statuesque he heard a voice and wondered if it could be from his owner's family. It wasn't a desire, just a curiosity. Again he wished he could feel. If he could feel he might desire to see his owners again. If he could feel he might come to think of them as his family, to love them.

As the two people approached he could make them out through the corner of his eye. He began mumbling as best he could with a frozen jaw to the girl and the scarecrow. Maybe he could care. Maybe if he had a heart.

The Tower

April reached for the spy glass. It had been years since she had thought to use it. It seemed to have some magical property that drew her to it when something approached.

Grasping it, she did not lift it immediately wondering if it were worth the effort. With a sigh, she carried it to the balcony and looked out over the dry scorched earth surrounding her tower. On all sides mountains loomed up.

After scanning the surroundings for several minutes, she saw it. A small dust cloud rose from the plain some miles away. Bringing up the spy glass she focused in on a knight, trotting in on a white horse. He was too far away to make out his features, but she imagined him to be handsome and strong, brave and true.

Lowering the glass she turned and started straightening up the room, making the bed, putting books back on their shelves, and quickly sweeping the floor.

Turning to the magical tray that provided food and drink she ordered up some fruits, cheese, bread and wine. He would be tired and need refreshment. Once everything seemed perfect she sat and ate a few grapes while waiting.

After what seemed like hours the door to her tower room burst open and in strode a tall, well-muscled man with bright blue eyes and soft wavy brown hair. His sword was brandished before him and his eyes darting about the room.

April stood. "Welcome," she said.

"Where is it?" he hissed.

"Where is what?" she responded with a sigh, hoping it wasn't what she knew he must be talking about.

"The beast, the demon, the…" he stammered. After a moment he seemed to get his words back. "That which keeps you trapped in this tower. I must vanquish it and free you from its evil hold."

He continued to search the room with his eyes and then spun about quickly to face something that might have crept up behind him. Nothing was there.

April cleared her throat and the knight turned to face her.

"No, sorry, only me." She gestured to the table. "Please come and refresh yourself."

He looked at the tray of food and then at April again. "So, um, there's no dragon?"

"No dragon."

His shoulders seemed to droop. "No troll or witch?"

She shook her head.

"Not even a crazed wood cutter?"

"Sorry, fresh out."

She gestured to the tray again. "Now, please come, eat and drink. You must be famished."

Straightening himself up he said, "No, I have come to rescue you. Come with me now and I'll take you away from this, to live in my castle, to be princess and eventually queen of all Elder Branch."

"Well," she said tentatively. "I was thinking that maybe you'd want to stay here with me?"

"I'm sorry, what?" he asked, his face all screwed up.

"You see this is my home. It's nice comfortable and safe. She stepped closer. "And with love's first kiss we can be safe here forever." She smiled and stretched out her arms.

"Here?" he asked looking around the room again.

"Look, no monsters or beasts ever come here; it will be a safe environment to raise our children."

"But, I, well, you know," he stammered again. "I'm a knight. I must go off to right wrongs, to vanquish evil and kill monsters."

"What," she raised her voice, "and I'm to sit at home wondering if you're lying dead in some foreign land, or that you'll come home horribly maimed, and I'll nurse you for the rest of your days? No, thanks."

April walked up to him and took his hand. "Please stay here with me." Again she smiled and batted her eyes for effect.

He drew back, eyes open wide. Bringing up

his sword, he thrust it between the two of them placing the tip at the nape of her neck. "Back you evil siren!" he yelled. "You will not lure me into your trap."

With that he ran from the room.

From the balcony she watched as the dust cloud disappeared into the distance. Using a small chisel she scraped a sixth mark on the railing. "Men," she said shaking her head.

Afterlife

"It was Joe's fault," the voice said.

"Yeah," Anthony shook his head. "The pretty boy got all the glory."

"And you deserved it so much more."

"I led in scoring at the state final, but he made the tie breaking goal. So, he's the hero."

"It's so unfair. He got your scholarship, didn't he?"

"Man, my life, it would have been so different, but he stole the best. It was Joe who kept me down."

"That's right, you would have had a better wife."

"Julie," Anthony saw her standing in front of him. He lifted his arms to reach her, but his fingertips fell an inch short. He stretched further and it made no difference. "Is that you?"

Ghostly images of women spread from his arms. Their distorted faces were familiar to him.

"A better wife would have made the difference. One who could understand your loneliness. She drove you to the other women."

Anthony waved his arms, attempting to beat away the specters. They grew into a haze, swirling around his arms. Julie was lost in the fog. When it lifted, she was gone. He wanted to cry. His eyes burned, but nothing came out. "Please, a drink?"

"Then she judged you, Anthony the adulterer. How unfair, how unjust. You deserved better."

Anthony's body burned, like it was on fire. He reached up to wipe the sweat from his brow, and found it dry. He swallowed, like dust going down a dry hole.

"But, Sara was different. Your beautiful daughter didn't judge you."

"No, please don't," he begged the voice.

"You were an excellent father, loving, caring, a good role model. It's not your fault."

"Stop! Stop!"he screamed at the top of his lungs.

"Remember her pretty face. There wasn't much left after the accident."

Anthony began clawing at his face and neck, trying to rip the flesh off. He could tear out a vein, or bleed to death. Anything to end it, anything. It didn't work; not a mark, not a scratch, not even pain.

"She was drunk on liquor from your cabinet when she hit the tree. You had no way to control her. It wasn't your example that brought her to that end. It must have been her friends. You loved her. You wouldn't have done that to her!"

Anthony fell to his knees and opened his arms to what would be the sky.

"Sara, I'm sorry. I'm so very sorry."

"Now she's up there and you're down here.

It's just not fair, is it?"

"Sara!"he called. "Sara!"

"Let's go over it again shall we?"

"No," he screamed, jumping to his feet. "Not again, not ever!" He grasped at the air, trying to rip the voice from it. He must stop the voice. He had to stop the voice. He knew that he could, somehow, because it was his own voice.

"It was Joe's fault," the voice said.

ABOUT THE AUTHOR

Timothy O. Goyette lives in New Hampshire and is the editor of the web-zine Quantum Muse. Many of his short stories can be found there.

If you want to give something longer a try, pick up Tim's Science Fiction novel: Lockdown.